P9-CRM-504

The FIREFIGHTER
Bernice Thurman Hunter

Cover photo by
Wayne Sproul/AGS Photography

Scholastic Canada Ltd.

Other Scholastic titles by the same author:
The Railroader
Lamplighter
That Scatterbrain Booky
With Love from Booky
As Ever, Booky
A Place for Margaret
Margaret in the Middle
Margaret on her Way

To Joe and Yvonne, for their help and friendship.

We gratefully acknowledge the Toronto Fire Department for their assistance and advice in the preparation of this book.

Scholastic Canada Ltd.
123 Newkirk Road, Richmond Hill, Ontario, Canada L4C 3G5

Scholastic Inc.
730 Broadway, New York, NY 10003, USA

Ashton Scholastic Limited
Private Bag 1, Penrose, Auckland, New Zealand

Ashton Scholastic Pty Limited
PO Box 579, Gosford, NSW 2250, Australia

Scholastic Publications Ltd.
Villiers House, Clarendon Avenue, Leamington Spa
Warwickshire CV32 5PR, UK

Thanks to Arbeiter's Envy Me of Tashdala ("Abby") and her owner, Carol Wilson, and to Captain William Adams and the A-2 Shift at Fire Station 8, for their help with our cover photo.

Photographs on pages vi , 16, 68, 90, and 119 reproduced by permission of the Toronto Fire Department. Photograph on page 160 by Wayne Sproul/AGS Photography.

Canadian Cataloguing in Publication Data

Hunter, Bernice Thurman
     The firefighter

ISBN 0-590-74051-2

I. Title.

PS8565.U57F5 1991   jC813'.54   C91-094303-6
PZ7.H85Fi 1991

Copyright © 1991 by Bernice Thurman Hunter. All rights reserved. No part of this publication may be reproduced or stored in a retrieval system, or transmitted in any form or by any means, electronic, mechanical, photocopying, recording, or otherwise, without written permission of the publisher, Scholastic Canada Ltd.

6 5 4 3 2 1   Printed in Canada   1 2 3 4 5 6/9
                      Manufactured by Gagné Printing

Contents

Chapter 1

The Anniversary

Terry Dawson sat on the top step of the veranda of the house on Ossington Avenue, elbows on knees, chin propped in his hands. He knew that if he let himself think about the terrible thing that had happened exactly one year ago he would probably cry.

Suddenly the sound of screaming sirens and clanging bells jerked him to attention. Jumping up, he leapt down the steps, grabbed his bike from where he'd thrown it on the lawn, and went whizzing up the street toward the firehall.

It was a two alarmer — a big one. The firemen, in their black leather helmets, white-striped black coats and black rubber boots, swung onto the backs of the gleaming red fire trucks as they careered out of Firehall 14 and went speeding along Bloor Street.

Terry pedalled furiously after them, his legs pumping a mile a minute. Up ahead he could see black smoke billowing over the rooftops. Filled with an indescribable excitement, he arrived red-faced and panting at the scene just minutes after the fire trucks.

Already the extension ladder had been propped against an upstairs window sill. Fiery smoke poured from the broken window, swirling above the fireman's head. Other firefighters manned the hoses. Still more forced the front door open, to be instantly engulfed in a rolling black cloud.

An ambulance arrived, red lights flashing, siren wailing. A crowd of neighbours wrung their hands and murmured together.

Moments later a man and a woman were carried, choking and gasping, out the front door of the blazing house and placed on stretchers. The woman was crying, "My baby! My baby!" as a neighbour in a housecoat knelt to comfort her. Sympathetic eyes looked down at the pain-filled faces, then shifted to the upstairs window.

A cheer went up as a fireman appeared in the opening and handed a small bundle wrapped in a blue blanket into the waiting arms of his mate perched on top of the ladder.

A man in shirt sleeves cupped his hands around

his mouth and shouted, "Nobody else in there! Get out and save yourself!" But the fireman's masked face disappeared back into the inferno.

Minutes dragged by like hours. The crowd was still with fear. "The damn fool!" declared the man in shirt sleeves. But Terry knew that every room in the house had to be searched before the fireman could think about his own safety.

Glowing embers flitted through the air like fireflies. Terry brushed them out of his dark curly hair. A woman began to pray out loud and other people joined her. As if in answer to their petition, the fireman emerged through the smoke-filled doorway. He pulled off his mask, his white teeth gleaming against his blackened face. In one arm he cradled a mewling, sooty white cat.

Leaning forward on the handlebars of his bike, Terry hung around until the fire was completely out. He watched eagerly as the fire-crew, supervised by their captain (Terry recognized him by the shield on his helmet), tar-papered the broken windows and boarded up the doors. Then they began rolling up the hoses.

Terry glanced at his wristwatch, a Bulova his dad and mom had given him on his eleventh birthday. It was five o'clock. He had been gone nearly two hours. Reluctantly he left the fire scene and began pedalling slowly back. As the excitement of the fire wore off, reality returned.

One year ago this very day Terry's whole life had changed forever. It had happened September 6, 1954. Labour Day. His parents and his little brother, Albert, had gone to visit friends at their summer cottage. Terry had begged not to go this one time. There were no kids his age at the cottage that summer, and besides, his best friend Frankie Weir had invited him to stay with his family for the weekend. It had taken a lot of fast talking to persuade Terry's mother, but she had finally given in.

On the way home from the cottage that night, there had been a terrible accident. A huge tractor-trailer jack-knifed on the highway, crushing the Dawsons' little green Volkswagen. Through a haze of grief and disbelief Terry learned that his parents had been so badly injured that their coffins would have to be closed. But four-year-old Albert's body had come through the horrendous crash unmarked. His little white casket would be open from head to toe.

Terry could see him yet, in his navy-blue sailor suit with short pants, white ribbed stockings with no shoes; that small waxen face and stiff little fingers wrapped around a bunch of forget-me-nots. How he wished he'd been with them! A lump as hard as a peach stone rose in his throat as he thought about it. He swallowed painfully as he wheeled his way towards home.

Chapter 2

The House on Ossington

Home, if you could call it that, was the house on Ossington just below Bloor Street. He had been living there for three months now. Before that he had been shunted around from one foster home to another. Finally Aunt Lottie and Aunt Betty, his only living relatives, had taken him in.

Charlotte and Elizabeth Dawson were his father's sisters. They were spinsters who, in spite of their differences — Charlotte was tall, dark and irascible, while Elizabeth was short, fair and sweet-natured — had been living together amicably for twenty-five years.

Terry knew that they had agonized over what to do with him. He had eavesdropped the day they came to discuss his future with his last foster mother.

"We are very set in our ways," he had heard his Aunt Lottie say in the nasal tone that set his teeth on edge like the scraping of fingernails on a blackboard, "and we don't particularly like children. Especially boys." Then Aunt Betty had piped up in the chirpy voice that always reminded him of an excited sparrow. "Speak for yourself, Charlotte. I do like children. Especially boys." And she had pointed out, more soberly, their duty towards their dead brother.

That last remark had obviously pricked Aunt Lottie's conscience. She prided herself on always doing her duty. Terry knew darned well that's what he was — a duty, a royal pain-in-the-neck.

* * *

He came in the back door more quietly than usual and caught Aunt Betty red-handed, puffing on an Export cigarette.

"For mercy sakes, child, you startled me!" Her heart-shaped face flushed and she laughed as she took one more drag, blew the smoke out her button nose, and ran the burning tip of the cigarette under the kitchen tap. Then she hid the evidence at the bottom of the garbage pail. "Wipe your feet, Terry," she said as she fanned the smoke out the door. "You look a sight. Where have you been?"

She glanced at the rooster clock on the wall,

then began scurrying around, setting the table.

"To a fire," he answered, scraping his shoes on the doormat. "A big one over on Gladstone Avenue. You should have seen it, Aunt Betty. It was magnificent."

She paused with three blue-willow plates in her plump hands and looked at him with his father's twinkly blue eyes. "Was anyone hurt?" she asked anxiously.

"I dunno. They took three people away in an ambulance. But a fireman saved a little old white cat."

"Well, magnificent doesn't seem to be the appropriate word then, Terry. Let's hope more than the cat escaped harm." She filled the whistling teakettle at the sink, put it on the stove and turned on the gas. Blue flames licked up the sides of the copper kettle. She turned the knob to low. "We'll have to watch the six o'clock news on the Admiral and find out what happened," she said.

The ten-inch black-and-white Admiral television set was an old one which they used very sparingly to save on the picture tube.

Aunt Betty shuffled the plates around on the yellow Arborite tabletop and set paper napkins under each fork. "Get washed before your Aunt Lottie comes home from work," she suggested.

Charlotte Dawson ran the family business on Bloor Street. Her father, Terry's grandfather, had opened The Fancy Floral Shoppe some forty years ago and when he died Charlotte, his eldest child, had taken over.

Just then they heard the click of the front door, a pause, which meant Aunt Lottie was hanging up her hat and coat on the wall hanger, then the clumping of rubber heels on hardwood. "Speak of the devil," Aunt Betty murmured.

Charlotte Dawson marched into the kitchen, set a Hunt's bakery box tied with string on the corner of the table, and hung her handbag on the broom closet doorknob. Flaring her long, thin nostrils, she sniffed the air suspiciously. "Have you been smoking, Terence?" she demanded.

"No, I been to a fire," he said quickly, with a glance at Aunt Betty.

"Well, get yourself straight upstairs into the bathtub. And change every stitch of clothes. I couldn't eat a bite with that smell."

Terry left the room without answering. He detested his Aunt Lottie. She stinks like peat moss and manure, and she needs a bath worse than I do, he thought. If it weren't for Aunt Betty . . .

The bathtub was the old-fashioned kind with lion's paws for feet. He turned on both taps full blast and got undressed. "Heck, I just got a bath yesterday. I'm not even dirty," he grumbled. So he skipped the soap, splashed around for ten seconds, then jumped out and rubbed himself dry on a pink towel. That was a mistake, he realized. There was a brown towel meant for him hanging on the rack. Now the pink one was covered in grey smudges. Aunt Lottie would throw a fit if she found it, so he rolled it up inside his sooty clothes and stuffed the whole kit and caboodle under the laundry already in the white wicker hamper. Then he streaked, stark naked, up the attic stairs.

That was the one thing he really liked about the house on Ossington: his attic bedroom. It was a big room that took up the whole third floor. It had sloping ceilings supported by wooden beams, a dormer window that looked out over the big oak tree on the front lawn, and a casement window that overlooked the backyard.

There wasn't much furniture in the room. The attic had been full of junk when Terry moved in. His aunts had put the junk in the cellar and furnished the room with odds and ends: a wooden wardrobe, a bureau for his clothes, and a narrow cot. On the night table beside the cot was a lamp that Terry's grandfather had made from a green glass decanter.

He dressed in clean clothes, combed his short curly black hair in front of the bureau mirror, and went downstairs.

As Terry slipped into his place at the table he saw that his plate was already full. He grabbed his fork and dug right in.

Aunt Lottie cleared her throat meaningfully. Terry glanced up. Both women sat with their hands clasped over their steaming plates, staring at him. Aunt Betty's golden eyelashes were fluttering like a butterfly's wings, as if she were trying to tell him something. But what?

Aunt Lottie cleared her throat again, and Terry dropped his fork nervously. It fell with a clatter to the floor. Terry leaned down, retrieved it with two fingers and was about to dig in again when Aunt Lottie's long arm shot out and snatched the fork from his hand. She made a great ceremony of taking it to the sink and dropping it with a plop into the dishpan. Then she sat down, got him a clean fork from the table drawer, clasped her hands again, and waited.

Terry looked from one face to the other. Now Aunt Betty's fair eyebrows were knitted together as tight as stitchwork across the bridge of her snub nose. She winked surreptitiously. Finally he got the message. It was his turn to say the blessing.

His mind was so full of other things this day that he couldn't remember any of the blessings his mother had taught him at home, so long ago. At last he mumbled the only words he could think of, a prayer he'd heard a preacher say once.

"Thanks be to thee for this our life; deliver us from woe and strife, Amen." He knew it wasn't a proper grace, but he hoped it would do.

"Amen," breathed Aunt Betty thankfully.

"Amen," added Aunt Lottie grudgingly.

Without lifting his eyes from his plate, Terry began to eat. Aunt Betty's shepherd's pie was his favourite dish. She made it with kernel corn because she knew he hated peas. Aunt Lottie said, "Spoil the boy, and you spoil the man." Whatever that meant.

But today even his favourite dish didn't tempt him. Suddenly Terry had lost his appetite. The thrill of the fire was long past and in its place came the awful recollection of the tragedy that had changed his life.

Didn't they remember at all, these two sisters of his father? He glanced up from under dark-winged eyebrows and saw a tear curving over Aunt Betty's round cheek. Then a shadow crossed Aunt Lottie's long face. "Labour Day," she said in a hollow voice. "I'm glad it's come and gone."

So they did remember.

Still, he wished that his spinster aunts had been spinster uncles. At least one of them.

Chapter 3

Playing Hooky

When Terry had lived at home with his mom and dad and Albert he had been considered a pretty good kid. But now it seemed like he was always getting into trouble.

Once he had liked school, but after going to three different ones in one year he hated it. When he had been in the foster homes he had often skipped half-days, written his own notes, and gotten away with it.

One warm Indian summer day he decided to try it again. The dollar bill Aunt Betty had given him for cleaning the leaves and little tree-sprouts out of the veranda eavestroughs was burning a hole in his pocket. (Aunt Lottie said he shouldn't be paid for chores, that it was the least he could do for his keep, but Aunt Betty always gave him a dollar anyway.)

So after lunch, instead of going back to school, he went downtown to the show. John Wayne was in a swell western at the Imperial, and to top it off the newsreel showed a raging fire that had recently demolished a huge cathedral in New York City.

Terry leaned forward eagerly in his seat, fascinated as always by a fiery spectacle. Bright orange flames leapt out of the church windows. They looked so real that he imagined he could feel the heat on his face, and he half-expected the theatre curtains to catch fire.

The camera zoomed in on two firefighters emerging like black ghosts through the charred cathedral doors. Right away Terry noticed that they had their helmets on backwards. He made a mental note to ask Firefighter Joe Hancock about it.

Joe was his friend at Fire Station 14, and Terry's hero. Unlike John Wayne, Joe didn't have daredevil stuntmen to do his dirty work. Terry had often seen Joe and his mates climbing up the precarious aerial ladders high above a burning building.

Terry left the theatre in good spirits and managed to get home about the same time as if he'd been at school.

After supper, Aunt Lottie asked him to post a letter for her at the corner mailbox. Terry loped off up the street, but instead of dropping the letter

through the slot he folded it in half and fitted it into his back pocket. Then he headed for the firehall.

The clock in the high tower struck seven. The two big doors were rolled up and the red fire trucks, gleaming under the lights, faced the street ready for action. A fireman Terry didn't recognize was polishing the chrome on the headlamps with a chamois, and Joe Hancock was reading a newspaper, his chair tipped back against the wall. When he saw Terry he folded the paper and let the chair come forward with a whack.

"Hello, there, son!" he said with a wide smile that stretched his thick brown moustache.

Terry felt his heart tighten in his chest. The last person who'd called him "son" was his father. "Mind your p's and q's, son," he had said as he left for the cottage that fateful weekend, "and don't give Mrs. Weir any trouble."

Joe looked at him quizzically. "Is there anything wrong?" he asked kindly.

Terry blinked. "Oh, no. I just come to ask you something."

"Fire away."

So Terry told him about the newsreel and how he'd noticed that the firemen's helmets were on backwards. Joe laughed and took down his own helmet from a hook on the wall. "Not many laymen would have noticed that," he remarked, holding the hard leather hat between his hands. "You see how the brim slopes down at the back? It forms a trough to let the water run off." Then he turned it around. "Now, when you wear it backwards the trough acts as a shield to protect your face against the heat. Here, you try it."

He set the leather helmet on Terry's dark curly head. It was so big it came down over his ears. Terry turned it around like a bowl. "It sure is heavy," he laughed.

He was interrupted by a loud voice coming down from the hole in the ceiling that the fire pole ran through.

Terry would have given anything to slide down that pole, but Joe had explained that it was against regulations to let anyone but a fireman use it. If you hadn't been taught to do it right, he said, you could easily break your ankle.

"Hey, you, Buck!" The voice of Firefighter Bill Collins bellowed from the room above. "How's about a game of dominoes?"

"Be right with you!" Joe called back. He took the hat off Terry's head and returned it to the line of black helmets and white-striped black canvas coats hanging in a row on the wall. Terry noticed the white helmet and yellow coat on the end hook.

"I guess it's time you were running along, son," Joe said.

"Okay, but can I ask a couple more questions?"

"Make it quick." Joe already had his foot on the bottom stair.

"Whose outfit is that?" Terry pointed to the yellow coat and white helmet on the end hook.

"Oh, that belongs to Sparkey, our District Fire Chief," explained Joe.

"Why do you call him Sparkey?"

"Because he's got a real thing about stamping out every last spark."

"You coming, Buck?" came the voice from up top again.

"Be right there," Joe answered.

"How come he calls you Buck instead of Joe?" Terry persisted.

The fireman's moustache stretched in a grin again. "That's my nickname. We all have nicknames in the Department. Bill up there is known as Old Leather Lungs."

"How come you call him that?"

"Because his lungs have been 'tanned' so often they're tough as leather. See you around, son." Waving Terry toward the door, Joe disappeared up the staircase.

* * *

That night in the privacy of his attic room Terry practiced copying Aunt Lottie's handwriting from the back of the envelope. She wrote in long, bold strokes. Her signature was the hardest part because of the way she swirled the C and made long tails on her S's. He rewrote the note several times. "Dear Mr. Snarr," it read. "Terence was absent from school yesterday afternoon because he suffered a seering migrain headache," Terry knew migraines were searing because Aunt Lottie got them about once a month and she nearly went crazy with the pain, "so I thought it wise to keep him home. Yours truly, Charlotte S. Dawson." He considered a minute, then added, "Proprietor of Dawson's Fancy Floral Shoppe." That sounded pretty impressive.

Terry re-read the note several times. It was just about perfect, he thought, so he folded it carefully and put it, with the envelope, back into his pocket. Then he climbed into bed, switched off the green bottle lamp, and went to sleep. The next morning he posted the letter and handed the note to Mr. Snarr.

* * *

After school Terry rode home with his new friend, Eric Thurston. Well, maybe Eric wasn't exactly a friend, but he lived on the same street and was in Terry's class at school.

Frankie Weir had been his best friend. A real pal. A guy you could trust. But he lived too far away now and the Weirs didn't even have a phone so Terry had lost touch with him.

Eric was different. You couldn't trust him as far as you could spit. He was always snitching and getting guys in trouble. Terry didn't like him nearly as much as Frankie, but he was somebody to hang around with.

The two boys stopped in front of the Thurstons' house and stood astride their bikes for a minute, talking. Then Eric's mother called, and Terry went home.

He was whistling out of tune (his mother always used to tease him about his tin ear) as he ran up the porch steps and into the kitchen.

Chapter 4

Forgery!

One look at Aunt Betty's stricken face and the whistle died in Terry's throat. And the presence of Aunt Lottie, home an hour early from the shop, made his heart do somersaults.

She towered over him, stiff as a ramrod, hands on hips, and glared down at him with steely eyes. "I had a phone call at my place of business today . . . " instantly he knew it had been a mistake to identify the shop, "and you may be sure your sins have found you out." Her voice was as cold as her eyes. "You forged — *forged!* — my signature. And if it hadn't been for your atrocious spelling you might have gotten away with it. What a fine beginning for a life of crime!" She moved a step closer and Terry stumbled back. "Well? What have you got to say for yourself?"

He couldn't think of a thing to say for himself, so he muttered, "Nothing."

"Nothing! *Nothing!*" Aunt Lottie's hand shot out towards him.

Quick as lightning Aunt Betty stepped between them. Cupping his quivering chin in her hand she whispered, "Terry . . . say you're sorry and that you'll never do such a wicked thing again."

The hurt in her eyes bothered him more than Aunt Lottie's flinty glare. For her sake he said, "I'm sorry and I won't ever do it again."

Angry red patches burned on Aunt Lottie's high cheekbones. "Go to your room," she ordered fiercely, "and contemplate what your punishment should be." Then she snapped at his retreating back like a dog snapping at a postman's heels, "And don't you dare show your face for supper!"

Thankfully he reached his room and closed the attic door. It was no punishment to Terry to be sent to his room. It was his sanctuary. He liked to imagine, when he shut the door behind him, that he was alone in a cabin in the woods. The big oak tree outside the dormer window sounded wild and woodsy when the wind blew. Supper wasn't going to be a problem, either, because there was a long black licorice rope stashed under his pillow.

He flopped down on the bed and felt under the

pillow for the licorice. His eyes roamed around the room as he chewed. There were no pictures on the walls because the rafters sloped from the peaked roof to the foot-high baseboard. But a Maple Leaf Baseball pennant was thumbtacked just above his bed, and one picture in a gold frame sat on top of the bureau. It was a portrait of Terry's family. In the picture he was standing beside his dad with his hand on his dad's arm. Albert was sitting on their mother's lap. The picture had been taken just a month before the accident.

Suddenly Terry couldn't stand the happy smiles another second. He jumped off the bed and shoved the picture to the back of the top bureau drawer, underneath his shirts. He flopped back down again, scrubbing the wet from his eyes with his fists, and tore off another chunk of licorice with his strong white teeth.

There was no point contemplating his punishment. Aunt Lottie would decide that anyway. So Terry thought about the fire department instead. Being a firefighter must be the most exciting job in the world. He could hardly wait for his next visit to the firehall. He thought he wouldn't go again for a few days, though, because he didn't want Joe Hancock to get sick of him. He'd already noticed the other firemen at Station 14 giving him funny looks as if he'd been hanging around too much.

Suddenly his thoughts were interrupted by a scream that made his blood run cold. Throwing the licorice up in the air, he bounded from the bed and raced downstairs. There in the hallway stood his aunts, craning their necks upwards, staring mesmerized at something above their heads. He followed their gaze, squinting to see through the semi-darkness of the vaulted hall ceiling. There it was — a shadowy thing hanging upside-down from the dangling light fixture.

A bat! A real live bat!

"Holy cow!" breathed Terry.

"Shh!" hushed Aunt Betty.

"Phone the exterminators, Elizabeth," hissed Aunt Lottie.

"No, don't do that," protested Terry in a husky whisper. "They might kill it. I bet I could catch it if I had a net."

"Father's fishing net is still hanging under the alcove in the cellar," whispered Aunt Betty.

"Get it, Terence," commanded Aunt Lottie.

Stealthily he made his way to the cellar, found the net and returned to the hallway. Just at that moment Aunt Lottie let out a sneeze as sharp as a pistol shot. The bat took off like a kite in the wind, swooping and flapping in a wild frenzy.

Both aunts stumbled backwards into the dining room and shut the door. Then all went quiet. The bat had returned to the safety of the light fixture.

Trembling with excitement, Terry held the net above his head and kept his arms rigid and ready.

He heard the door ease open behind him and Aunt Betty whispered, "Be careful it doesn't get in your hair, Terry."

Good grief! he thought. Then Aunt Lottie sneezed again and with a terrified squeal the little wild creature dove, at incredible speed, straight into the fishing net.

Terry slammed the net to the floor. "I've got him! I've got him!" he yelled triumphantly. "Somebody bring me a dustpan!"

Aunt Betty rushed for the dustpan and Terry eased it under the net, trapping the bat inside. "Now open the front door," he ordered.

The two women bumped into each other in their hurry to fling open the door. Then they plastered themselves against the wall as Terry ran out onto the veranda with his terrified prisoner.

Leaning over the railing, he dropped the dustpan and shook the writhing, seething net as hard as he could.

Finally the animal got untangled and dropped like a stone to the ground. For a second it lay there, stunned. Then, suddenly realizing that it was free, it zoomed up into the air and disappeared over the treetops into the darkening sky.

The excitement over, Terry reluctantly went back inside and shut the door. Without speaking he returned the net to the cellar.

When he came back upstairs his aunts were in the kitchen. Aunt Betty had retrieved the dustpan and was hanging it on the nail in the broom closet.

Aunt Lottie cleared her throat. Then she said in a matter-of-fact tone of voice, "Get Terence his supper, Elizabeth, he must be starving."

Terry took that as a sure sign of forgiveness.

Chapter 5

The Punishment

The next morning Terry wasn't so sure. It was Saturday and he woke to the sound of fire-reels pealing past the house. Leaping out of bed, he dressed in a flash and flew down the two flights of stairs. He was brought up short by the sight of Aunt Lottie standing in the hallway pulling on her black kid gloves.

"Where do you think you're off to in such a hurry?" she asked, deftly blocking his attempt to duck under her arm.

"I want to see where the fire is. May I get past, please?"

"No, you may not. I have other plans for you today, young man. I need help in the back of the shop. I think you owe me that much, don't you?"

She couldn't have picked a better punishment if

she'd thought for a week. Aunt Lottie knew he hated The Fancy Floral Shoppe. Just the name of the place sent shivers like tiny spiders skittering all over his body. The overwhelming smell of plants and soil and peat moss, all blended together, made his stomach turn. Ever since the funeral he couldn't stand the sight of flowers. Especially forget-me-nots.

Aunt Betty appeared in the doorway, unpinning the pink mesh hairnet she wore at night. "Charlotte," she ventured, "I need Terry to steelwool the hardwood today."

"The floors can wait," her sister replied tartly. "The shop comes first and foremost."

"But I hate the smell," objected Terry.

"Well, the fragrance of flowers is not going to disappear from the face of the earth just to please you, young man. And it's high time you got over such nonsense before it becomes a full-blown phobia."

"But . . . " The wail of the siren was fast fading into the distance. Terry sighed.

"No buts. Go eat your breakfast. I'll expect you," she pushed up her coat sleeve and glanced at her round gold wristwatch, "at nine o'clock sharp." With that she turned on her heel and stalked out the door.

In the kitchen he drank his glass of orange juice as Aunt Betty scooped a big spoonful of Red River

Cereal into his bowl. Then she went to retrieve her package of Exports from behind the bread-tin.

Terry stirred milk into the cereal and sprinkled it with brown sugar. The radio jingle floated through his mind: "We all love Red River Cereal . . . it's made of the best material!" Normally he did love the crunchy brown nuggets, but today he wasn't hungry.

"She hates me!" he said, pushing his bowl away.

"Oh, Terry, no. Don't say that." Aunt Betty sat down beside him and flicked ashes into a saucer. "She's just overwrought, that's all. It isn't easy being the breadwinner in the family, you know. And the shop didn't get its excellent reputation by accident. Your Aunt Lottie earned it through hard work, and it's up to us to help her all we can."

Terry knew she was right, but he frowned and muttered, "Well, I still think she's mean."

Aunt Betty took a long drag on her Export and blew twin puffs out her nose. "No, Terry. She's not mean. She's strict, I'll grant you, and she's got old-fashioned ideas about child-rearing. But she always tries to be fair."

Still unconvinced, Terry left his breakfast half-eaten, got his windbreaker from the hook on the porch wall, and went out the back door.

He wished he could run away, but he didn't have

enough money saved up. That's what he'd do, he thought with sudden resolve. He'd save every cent from now on until he had fifty dollars. Aunt Betty usually slipped him a dollar when he did chores, and the firemen at Station 14 often gave him a quarter to run errands since they weren't allowed to leave their posts. If he saved it all he'd soon have fifty dollars. Then he'd head for South America — nobody would think to look for him there. Besides he was sure, in spite of what Aunt Betty said, that Aunt Lottie would be glad if he disappeared forever.

* * *

The little brass bell on the door of The Fancy Floral Shoppe jingled as Terry entered. Instantly the heady fragrance overwhelmed him. He gagged and was suddenly glad he hadn't eaten all his breakfast.

Aunt Lottie appeared in the doorway of the back room with pruning shears in one hand and a bunch of long-stemmed roses in the other. "Come out here, Terence," she said, her voice a little more pleasant now.

The back room was thick with green foliage; spider plants and creeping vines hung in wicker baskets from the low-beamed ceiling. The earthy smells caught in his throat, taking his breath away.

"I've got two funeral wreaths and a wedding bouquet that must be ready by noon. So the first thing I want you to do is to unpack these green boxes. Fill the buckets half-full of water and put each variety of flower in a separate bucket. Then clean up the debris."

The bell jingled again, so she set the shears and roses on the work table, stroked back her short brown hair, and hurried to the counter to wait on her client. (That was what Aunt Lottie always called her customers.)

With the point of the shears, Terry began slitting open the green boxes. Each contained a different kind of flower: chrysanthemums, irises, lilies, roses . . . forget-me-nots. The sight of the little blue flowers made his stomach heave again. Turning quickly away, he grabbed the metal pails off the floor and hurried to the sink for water. Then he trimmed the stems and filled each pail with blossoms.

When he was finished he noticed a long brown box tied with green string at the back of the work table. Aunt Lottie hadn't told what it was, but he decided to open it anyway. He snipped the string and lifted the lid.

The contents made Terry gasp in horror. Packed precisely, row on row, were wide pastel ribbons, pink and white and blue and beige, each glittering with gold or silver lettering: Mother, Father, Sister,

Brother. The words pierced his heart. He smashed the lid back on and threw the box under the table.

Quickly he grabbed up the long-handled broom that leaned in the corner and began sweeping frantically into every nook and cranny. Twigs and leaves and moss and dirt flew like a whirlwind into a pile in the middle of the floor. Then he shovelled the musky mound into a trash can and lugged it out the back door.

Next he lined up the buckets of brightly coloured blossoms against the wall. They reminded him painfully of the profusion of flowers at the funeral home. He jerked his eyes away and found other chores to do.

The doorbell had been ringing constantly all morning long so it was half past eleven before his aunt came back to check on him.

"Why, Terence," she said, her eyes sweeping the room as clean as the cornbroom. "I can't get over it. The place has never looked so tidy. You've earned the rest of the day off." The bell jangled again, calling her back to the shop.

Terry stared after her in amazement. Praise from Aunt Lottie? He couldn't believe his ears.

He washed his hands at the sink, ran wet fingers through his hair to sift the dust out, and shrugged into his windbreaker. He was on his way out the delivery door when his aunt called him back.

"Don't tell me she's found another job for me to do," he grumbled as he made his way through the store toward her.

Charlotte Dawson was standing behind the counter at the cash register. She punched a key to open the drawer. Extracting a two-dollar bill, she snapped it between her fingers and handed it to her nephew.

Terry stared in amazement — she'd never paid him for helping in the shop before. "I haven't got any change, Aunt Lottie," he blurted.

She chuckled and Terry realized that was another first. He didn't remember ever hearing her laugh before.

Instantly she straightened her face and said brusquely, "Take it and be off with you before I change my mind."

"Thanks," he muttered as he folded the orange bill and stuffed it into his back pocket.

The bell jangled as he shut the door behind him. His bike leaned against the shop window. Swinging it around, he hopped on and went coasting along the sidewalk. Only forty-three more dollars to go, he thought gleefully, then South America here I come!

Chapter 6

Trash Fire!

Terry was standing on the back steps, reaching for the door, when he smelled smoke — acrid, smelly smoke like the stink of burning garbage. He looked down the back yard and saw a thin grey column of smoke floating over the flat rooftops of the garages and sheds that lined the laneway.

Instantly he leapt back down the steps, climbed the tall board fence separating their yard from the alley, and walked tightrope-style along the ledge. At the end of the fence he jumped off into the laneway.

The big trash dumpster behind their garden shed was engulfed in a thick black cloud. Suddenly it burst into a ball of orange flames.

"Holy smoke!" cried Terry as he sprinted up the alleyway towards the street. He ran to the corner and stopped in front of a fire-alarm box on a telephone pole. Behind the small glass window was the warning: "$50.00 Fine for False Alarm!" He hesitated for a split second, then picked up a stone, smashed the glass, and pulled the hook down.

Within a minute a fire truck with a five-man crew came pealing down Ossington from Station 14. The driver pulled up by the fire hydrant on the Dawsons' front lawn and one of the men leapt off the back to attach a hose to the hydrant. Then two others, Joe Hancock and a fireman Terry didn't know, slung the heavy hose over their shoulders and began hauling it down the laneway.

"Can I help, Joe?" begged Terry.

"Sure. Grab hold."

Terry put his shoulder under the huge hose and held it off the ground while the firefighters worked to douse the flames. In no time at all the fire was out.

Now the Captain turned to Terry. "Who turned in the alarm?" he wanted to know.

"Me . . . I did," replied Terry proudly.

The Captain narrowed his eyes and looked at Terry suspiciously. "Did you see who started it?" he asked.

"No, I didn't." There was a touch of defiance in Terry's voice. "I just came home from working at my aunt's shop and I smelled smoke — my nose is a good smoke detector — so I came out here to investigate. Then I set off the alarm."

"Well . . . no harm done this time. Could have been a lot worse. The wood in these old sheds is as dry as tinder. They're regular firetraps. Should be got rid of."

He took off his helmet and scratched his head as he scanned the laneway. Then he gave Terry a quizzical look that made him feel uneasy.

Apparently satisfied, Captain Forrest replaced his helmet and tapped it with his fingertips. Then he unbuckled his coat and pulled a handkerchief from his trouser pocket. Holding it over his mouth and nose like a mask, he peered into the steaming dumpster.

"What are you doing?" asked Terry curiously.

The Captain turned away from the dumpster and stuffed the handkerchief back into his pocket. "Well, it's my duty before I leave a fire scene to be sure that there's no chance of the blaze rekindling," he explained.

By now the hose was loaded back onto the fire truck, and Captain Forrest said to Terry, "I want you to keep your eyes peeled around here. We've had a lot of trash fires in this area lately. We could be dealing with a firebug." He strode towards the truck as he spoke. Terry lengthened his stride to match the Captain's.

"I'll keep a sharp lookout," he promised, his dark eyes flashing. "I like being a fire spotter."

Again the Captain shot him a keen glance. Then he shrugged and climbed into the cab beside his driver.

* * *

Aunt Betty stood on the top step of the porch, hugging herself inside her sweater coat. It was the middle of November and the air was chilly.

"What happened, Terry?" she asked as they went inside.

"Just a trash fire in the lane. Probably some old tramp threw a lighted butt into the dumpster. I set off the alarm." He went to the sink for a drink of water. "I wonder how long it takes to put new glass in the firebox?"

Aunt Betty was rummaging behind the bread tin in search of her cigarettes. "Oh, they'll have it replaced before you can say Jack Robinson," she assured him, taking a cork-tipped Export and placing it between her lips.

Terry struck a wooden match and lit the cigarette. Then he held the match downward and stared, fascinated, as the white flame crept up towards his fingertips. Suddenly he yelped in pain and dropped the match on the floor. He stamped it out and sucked his burnt finger. Then he dunked the blackened matchstick, with a little hiss, into a basin of water in the sink and hid it at the bottom of the garbage tin.

"Tsk! Tsk!" Aunt Betty chided, smoke drifting from her nostrils. "You shouldn't play with matches, Terry."

"Oh, yeah! Wait'll Aunt Lottie catches you in the act." He put his fingers to his lips and puffed on an imaginary cigarette.

"Well, don't hold your breath," Aunt Betty laughed, "because she phoned to say she was too busy to get home for lunch today." Saturday was the only day Lottie closed the shop for lunch.

They continued kidding each other as they ate their soup and sandwiches. Aunt Betty's a good sport, Terry thought. For a second he regretted his plan to run away.

After lunch he called on Eric Thurston and the two boys went down to Firehall 14 to see if they could make any money running errands. But this time Captain Forrest stopped them at the door and told them to shove off.

"What's eating him?" Eric asked as they pedalled away.

"I dunno," answered Terry. "But I gotta find a

way to earn some more money. I need fifty dollars and I only got seven."

"Whatcha need fifty dollars for?"

Terry glanced at Eric, remembering his reputation as a snitch. "I can't tell you," he finished lamely.

"So don't! Who cares!" snorted Eric.

Terry stood up on the pedals and put on a burst of speed. "Race you to the school yard," he yelled.

* * *

The minute Charlotte Dawson came in the door that evening she started wriggling her long, thin nose. "I smell smoke again!" she declared suspiciously.

A guilty look flitted across Aunt Betty's round face and Terry guessed that she had just doused another butt. He jumped to her defence. "The dumpster in the laneway caught fire this afternoon," he explained.

"I knew it!" Aunt Lottie bobbed her head triumphantly. "I've got an excellent sense of smell." Then she darted Terry a flinty glance. "Did you have anything to do with it?" she snapped.

"No! Well, I set off the fire alarm. And I helped get the blaze under control."

"I knew it! The nose knows!" Aunt Lottie smirked at her own joke. "Now, up the stairs you go, young man, and into the bathtub. You know I can't tolerate that stench while I'm eating."

Terry groaned as he clumped up the stairs to the bathroom. I wonder if I inherited her smeller, he thought disgustedly. If I did, I hope it's the only thing I got from the old witch.

He felt a sense of satisfaction when he called Aunt Lottie names. It was sort of like scratching an itch.

In the bathroom he turned both taps on full blast and poured in half a bottle of Aunt Betty's pink bubble bath. If he had to have a bath — and it was a wonder he had any skin left — it might as well be fun.

Sliding down into the tub until the pinky-white froth tickled his nose, he thought about Captain Forrest. "I wonder why he acted so funny with me today? I'll go up to the firehall after supper. Maybe Joe can tell me."

Chapter 7

Fire Station 14

One of the big firehall doors was rolled up so Terry walked in uninvited. The appetizing aroma of bacon and coffee came floating down through the hole in the ceiling. Some of the night crew must be up top cooking their dinner.

Joe was downstairs, inspecting the ladder on the aerial truck. He was whistling, "Chi-baba, chi-baba, chi-wawa," along with Perry Como's voice from the little mantle radio.

"Hi, Joe!" he yelled.

"Oh, hi there, son," Joe said.

Terry came closer and lowered his voice. "Is the captain here?" he asked, looking around.

"No, I'm in charge tonight. Is there anything I can do for you?"

"Oh, no," Terry shrugged. "I just thought you

might need something from the store."

"No, thanks just as much." Joe climbed into the cab and examined all the shiny gadgets on the instrument panel. Terry hopped up on the running board. "Can I sit in the cab with you?" he asked.

Joe shoved over. "Sure. Why not." he said.

Terry slid onto the black leather seat beside his hero. He stretched his arms around the huge steering wheel. "Boy, I'd sure like to drive this baby," he breathed.

Joe laughed as he checked the different gauges.

"Uh, can I talk to you about something, Joe?"

"Fire away."

Terry told him how the captain had been so abrupt with him and Eric that afternoon. "And we didn't do nothing," he complained.

Joe nodded knowingly. "That's just the captain's way. He doesn't mean anything by it. He's a pretty good egg, as long as you keep your nose clean."

Terry sighed with relief and sat back, enjoying the privilege of just being inside the fabulous fire truck. His dark eyes sparkled as they roved around the cab.

Joe began to polish the shiny instruments with a chamois, whistling away. Then all of a sudden he paused. "Terry, we've known each other for quite a while now, but you've never told me anything about your family. Have you got any brothers or sisters?"

Terry froze and his hands gripped the steering wheel so hard his knuckles turned white. The familiar lump swelled up in his throat and he knew he couldn't answer without crying. So he jumped down from the cab, ran out of the firehall, and sped away.

But he didn't go home. What kind of home did he have, anyway? Just a house where they bossed him around and made him work and get baths all the time.

He rode carelessly along Bloor Street, weaving in and out of traffic. Angry motorists blew their horns and shook their fists at him, but he didn't care. He rode around for about an hour, trying to get rid of the walnut-sized lump in his throat.

At last, tired and utterly forlorn, he headed for the only home he had . . . the house on Ossington.

Chapter 8

Blabbermouth

It was December, but instead of snowing it poured rain for days on end. Terry grew even more melancholy. One wet day Old "Snarkey" Snarr sprung a science test on the class. Terry groaned inwardly when he got his paper back and decided not to tell his aunts he had flunked. What they didn't know wouldn't hurt him, he reasoned. But Mr. Snarr collared him at the door before he could leave.

"Where are your books, Dawson?" he demanded.

"What books?" Terry asked insolently.

"What books, *sir!*"

"What books, *sir!*" mimicked Terry.

The teacher's eyes bulged. "Your science book for one. And geography and history and mathematics. With your marks you'll need them all. You haven't got a snowball's chance of passing your Christmas exams. And where is today's science test? You're to take it home and have it signed by both your parents . . . I mean both Miss Dawsons. I want them to know exactly where you stand."

Terry glowered at the floor. He went back to his desk, stuffed the test paper between the pages of his science book, grabbed it up, and made a beeline for the door. He could feel Mr. Snarr's bulgy eyes boring a hole in the back of his head.

Eric had stayed for basketball practice, so Terry walked home alone. By the time he reached the back porch he was soaked to the skin and the rain had tightened his hair up into little black corkscrews. He pulled his books out from inside his coat, hung up his windbreaker, kicked off his rubber boots and wandered into the kitchen in soggy socks.

Aunt Betty was busy making vanilla junket, dissolving two white tablets into a saucepan of warm milk. "For mercy sakes, child, get out of your wet things before you catch your death of cold," she scolded as she poured the mixture into sherbet glasses and carefully placed them on the counter to set. "Take all your wet clothes down to the cellar and hang them on the clotheshorse by the furnace."

Terry plunked his books on the table and slumped into a chair.

Aunt Betty began scrubbing potatoes with a wire brush. "Why are you just sitting there, Terry?" she asked. "I thought I told you to get changed." She dunked a potato in a pot of muddy water and glanced at her nephew. Seeing the dejected look on his face, her voice gentled. "Is there something troubling you, dear?" she asked.

He fished his test paper from the pages of his science book and held it out. Aunt Betty wiped her hands on her apron, then took it and scanned it from top to bottom. Then she shook her head in dismay. "Your Aunt Charlotte won't be happy about this," she said.

Terry sighed as he went upstairs, changed into dry clothes, and brought his wet things down to hang in the cellar.

Aunt Lottie looked surprised to find Terry immersed in homework at the dining room table. Aunt Betty had the kitchen table set and was busy dishing up the dinner. "Are you washed for supper, Terry?" she called.

It looked like she wasn't going to mention the paper until after supper, but Terry wanted to get it over with. He went to the kitchen cupboard where Aunt Betty had hidden it, retrieved it, and handed it to Aunt Lottie.

She read in stony silence, her thin lips pulled

down at the corners. Finally she looked up and their eyes met. With a sinking heart he listened to her edict.

"Every day, from now until Christmas, you will come straight home from school. You will study before supper; you will study after supper. No friends, no phone calls, and no television." Then, in exactly the same cold tone of voice, she thanked God for their supper.

The kitchen fell silent except for the odd scraping of cutlery on china. Terry forced down the meat and potatoes and said no thanks to the junket.

"Would you rather have a slice of apple pie, love?" coaxed Aunt Betty.

"With cheese?"

"That's pure extravagance, cheese on apple pie," declared Aunt Lottie.

"At home, my dad wouldn't eat apple pie without cheese," replied Terry obstinately.

Aunt Betty cut a generous slice of cheddar and laid it on a thick wedge of pie. Placing it in front of her nephew she said, "Apple pie without cheese is like a hug without a squeeze."

Terry laughed, and Aunt Lottie sighed. "Mother used to say that to Johnny when he was a boy," she murmured.

The days dragged by. Terry didn't miss the television much — he was hardly ever allowed to watch it anyway. He hardly missed Eric either. But every time the fire reels went pealing past the house he got madder and madder. He wasn't even allowed to run out on the street to see which direction the trucks were going.

Night after night he pored over his books, the anger building up inside him. He didn't care if he passed or not. All he wanted was to save enough money to run away.

Nearly every day Aunt Betty gave him a job to do. And when she paid him she always put a finger to her lips and said, "Mum's the word." Then she'd ask, "What's the matter, Terry?" and he'd always answer, "Nothing."

His little hoard of money grew. He had thirteen dollars and fifty cents now. Just thirty-six fifty to go. By the time spring came he should have enough. The idea was exciting, and Terry was dying to tell somebody.

"Can you keep a secret?" he asked Eric on the way home from school one day.

"Sure," promised Eric. "What's up?"

"Well, pretty soon, maybe as soon as Easter, I'm heading for South America."

Eric whistled at the news. "Where'll you get the dough?"

"I'll have it by then but don't ask me how."

"How?"

"Have you got wax in your ears? I said, don't ask."

"Ahhh, you're full of bull," sneered Eric.

They exchanged a few more insults before parting.

A couple of hours later Terry was back at the dining table doing his never-ending homework when the front door banged open and Aunt Lottie came flying in without even stopping to take off her slushy galoshes.

Grabbing her nephew by the scruff of the neck she jerked him to his feet. "You ungrateful little beast!" she hissed, shaking him like a cat. "How dare you plan to run away from the perfectly good home we've provided for you?"

"How . . . how did you find out?" Terry cried.

"Never you mind how I found out. I'm only thankful that my poor dead brother isn't here to know what a disgrace you are to his name."

She couldn't have said anything worse. "I hate you, you mean old witch!" he screamed, and wrenching himself from her grasp he made a dash for the stairs.

There was a crash from the kitchen and Aunt Betty came running. "Terry! Terry!" she cried. Then she turned on her infuriated sister. "Charlotte, what have you done?"

Charlotte Dawson pushed past her and took off up the stairs after Terry.

Terry glanced over his shoulder, expecting to see his Aunt Betty. His eyes widened and he raced up to the attic, grabbed the bedroom chair, and swung it around in front of him.

Aunt Lottie's tall frame filled the doorway. She stood with arms tightly folded, her grey eyes as dark as a thundercloud.

"Give me your money!" she demanded.

"No!" His legs were shaking and he had to cling to the back of the chair for support, but he continued defiantly, "It's mine! I earned it!"

His aunt didn't move a muscle, but her face turned as white as lard. "We are not leaving this room until the money is in my hand." Then she added in a self-righteous tone, "I will take charge of it for you. It will be safe with me, since I am not a thief."

They continued the standoff for five long minutes. At last Terry's eyes fell, and he knew he was beaten. Slowly he came out from behind the chair. His feet dragged as he went to the dresser. He pulled open the drawer, reached under his shirts for his alley-bag, and held it out towards his aunt. She snatched it from him, wheeled around, and left him standing there.

That night Terry sat hunched up on the dormer window-seat, staring out at the black silhouette of the oak tree, trying to figure out how Aunt Lottie had got wind of his hoard of money.

A fire siren wailed in the distance. He wished he could answer its magic call.

Suddenly, like a lamp being switched on in his head, he knew what had happened. Eric! Why had he taken a chance on that big blabbermouth? And why hadn't he remembered that Mrs. Thurston and Aunt Lottie were friends?

"That does it!" Terry fumed as he threw himself onto his bed. "With friends like him, who needs enemies? From now on I'm gonna be a loner."

Chapter 9

The Search

The next two weeks were solid misery. Finally Terry made a decision. He would launch an all-out search for his money. He waited patiently for the right opportunity.

It came sooner than he expected. One afternoon he found a note propped up against a covered casserole on the kitchen table.

"Dear Terry," Aunt Betty's round handwriting read, "Set the table and put the macaroni and cheese in the oven (350 degrees) at five o'clock sharp. Your Aunt Charlotte and I had to go downtown on business. We'll be back about six. Love, Aunt B."

Terry began his search in the kitchen, scouring the cupboards, the broom closet, the refrigerator. He even opened the foil-wrapped packages in the little freezing compartment of the Coldspot. Nothing. Next he went to the dining room and emptied the buffet drawers. Still nothing. He was careful to put everything back in its place.

Suddenly the cuckoo clock went off, scaring the wits out of him. It cuckooed five times, reminding him to set the table and put the casserole in the oven.

Then Terry began to hurry, afraid his aunts might come home early. He raced up the stairs two at a time and stopped breathlessly outside Aunt Lottie's closed bedroom door. Maybe it was locked. He almost hoped it was. But when he turned the brass knob the door opened easily. He took a quick step backward, his skin prickling with guilt.

He'd never set foot inside Aunt Lottie's room before. Her door was always shut. Aunt Betty always left her door open, even when she hadn't made her bed. Aunt Lottie complained, but Elizabeth Dawson held her ground. Charlotte might be the breadwinner, she said, but her room was her own and she would keep it just as she pleased.

Terry stepped gingerly into Aunt Lottie's domain and stopped short in surprise. The matching curtains and bedspread were pink and frilly. The dresser scarf was trimmed with fancy lace. Standing on one end of the scarf was a lamp that looked like an old-fashioned lady in a hooped skirt. She held a parasol in her hand, with a light bulb underneath it. The room didn't seem to suit Aunt Lottie at all.

Suddenly he realized that he was wasting time. Feeling as guilty as a sneak-thief he began to search carefully through the dresser drawers. The thought of what Aunt Lottie would do if she caught him meddling with her things gave him goose-bumps.

The money wasn't in the drawers so he moved on to the clothes closet. He turned pockets inside out, dumped shoe boxes upside down, and ran his hands along the top shelf. No luck.

He got down on all fours and peered under the bed. Not even a dust-ball. The ivory clock on the night table read ten minutes to six. Terry rose to leave.

At the door he turned and let his eyes roam around the room to be sure he'd left no tell-tale signs. Slowly his gaze passed over the dresser top. Then he did a double take. The doll-lamp had a peculiar bump at the back of her hooped skirt. He picked her up by the neck and there it was — his money-bag! He snatched it up and set the lamp down too quickly. It teetered precariously, and Terry grabbed it just in time. With a pounding heart and a sigh of relief he backed out the door and drew it shut behind him, just as his aunts came flurrying into the downstairs hallway. He crept on tiptoe up the attic stairs and hid his precious hoard underneath his pillow.

Then he came down to the bathroom, washed noisily, flushed the toilet twice, and went downstairs whistling. Aunt Lottie darted him a suspicious look and he stopped abruptly. Aunt Betty greeted him with a sad smile as she set the casserole on a heat-pad in the centre of the kitchen table.

He slipped quietly into his place, avoiding their eyes by staring at the rooster clock on the wall. Aunt Betty folded her hands and nodded her fluffy fair head at him. He caught her cue, bowed his head, and said a proper blessing. Then he ate everything on his plate, helped with the dishes without being asked, and finally sat down at the dining room table with his books.

His good behaviour almost backfired. Both his aunts eyed him curiously.

"Are you feeling all right, Terry?" asked Aunt Betty.

"Sure," he assured her.

"Have you been up to something?" queried Aunt Lottie.

"Nope," he answered, hoping she didn't hear his heart go thump.

At last the clock cuckooed nine times. Terry yawned and stretched, stacked up his books, and wished his aunts a cheery goodnight.

He climbed into bed without undressing, turned out the bottle lamp, and waited with his eyes wide open. Gradually his sight adjusted to the darkness and he could see the sloping rafters.

The peal of a fire siren crept through the window, and Terry pictured the activity going on at Fire Station 14. The single siren told him that only one truck was involved. A small fire, he thought. I wonder if Joe is on duty tonight?

At last he heard his aunts come up the stairs. He heard running water, the snap of light switches, then a murmured, "Goodnight" and finally the click of Aunt Lottie's door.

It seemed like hours before Aunt Lottie's sonorous snores came rumbling up the heat pipes and through the attic register. He glanced at the wristwatch his parents had given him. The green luminescent dial read eleven-thirty. He got up cautiously to prevent the bedsprings from squeaking and pulled his rubber boots and windbreaker from the wardrobe. He wished he'd remembered to bring his winter boots and jacket up from the back porch.

Instead he yanked on two thick pullovers before

stuffing his arms into the windbreaker. He could hardly do the buttons up. Next he pushed his money-bag deep inside a pocket, buttoned the flap, and grabbed two Sweet Marie bars that he'd been saving for an emergency. Easing open his sock drawer, he found a woollen toque and mitts and chose an extra pair of socks. At last he was ready.

The casement window that looked out onto the backyard opened smoothly on its track. Then a sudden gust of wind blew in and sent the green glass bottle lamp crashing to the floor. Amazingly, it didn't break, but the noise it made sounded like a shotgun blast.

Terry held his breath and listened, but all he could hear was his own blood pulsing through his veins. He began to count: "One thousand, two thousand, three thousand . . ." For a full minute he stayed perfectly still.

The house was as quiet as a graveyard. Then all of a sudden the silence was shattered by a loud, guttural, gurgling gasp, followed by an eerie silence.

Terry had heard the unearthly noise before and knew what it was, but it still sent cold shivers up his spine. Aunt Lottie was one of those weird people who stop breathing, sometimes for a whole minute, while they are sound asleep.

He started counting again. "One thousand . . . two thousand . . . three thousand . . ." Suddenly she exhaled and air belched out of her like the roar of a lion.

It was time to leave.

Bolted securely to the house right beside the back window was a steel television tower which made a perfect ladder to the ground. Terry had climbed up and down it before, just for fun. Easing himself backward over the ledge, he got a good grip on a rung of the tower. Then he drew the casement window almost shut behind him and began to descend.

The minute his feet touched the ground he was off and running.

Chapter 10

The Runaway

Bloor Street was alive with people swarming out of the late show. A popcorn machine was merrily showering little white clouds inside a big glass box as people lined up to insert a nickel in the slot. A white paper bag dropped from a bottom spout and filled magically with hot buttered popcorn. Terry slipped a nickel out of his pocket and waited his turn.

Munching on the greasy kernels, he strolled along with the crowd. The store windows sparkled with red and green lights. Terry had almost forgotten it was nearly Christmas. There wasn't a sign of the holiday spirit in the house on Ossington.

A gaily decorated tree in the window of the five and dime store caused a sudden picture of Christmases past to flash through his mind: the tree glittering with tinsel; his dad testing the string of lights, finding a bad one, replacing it, then plugging it in; Albert squealing with glee as the rainbow of colours snaked across the floor. Terry shook his head to rid himself of the painful memories.

The crowd had begun to thin out and the air was getting colder. Fine snow, sifting along on an east wind, swirled around a street light like a swarm of mosquitoes.

Suddenly a man staggered out from a dark alleyway.

"Hey, you, kid!" he yelled. "Got a dime for an old soldier?" His words were slurred and he was swaying drunkenly.

"I got no money," Terry said, backing away.

"Don't gimme that, kid," the man sneered, showing broken teeth in a red, bewhiskered face.

Terry turned and ran. Half a block away he glanced over his shoulder. He saw the man clinging to a lamppost so he slowed to a walk. He was back at the corner of Ossington and Bloor. He could just make out the hands of the clock in the tower of Fire Station 14. It was twelve-thirty.

Suddenly Terry felt very tired. He looked longingly at the firehall. It would be nice and warm in there. If only he could curl up on the black leather seat of a fire truck and go to sleep. But he knew that the night crew would be on the alert. Firemen took turns catnapping.

Bloor Street was deserted now. No, not quite. Someone was emerging through the mist of snow. A man in uniform. A cop! Where could he hide? Terry was just about to dash down the lane behind the firehouse when he heard the familiar ding, ding, ding of an approaching streetcar. He stepped out onto the road and waved frantically. The streetcar squealed to a stop and the doors clunked open. Terry hopped up the high steps into the warmth and light.

Taking the seat behind the driver, he felt in his money bag for a ten-cent piece to put in the fare box. The driver depressed the lever and the little trapdoor at the bottom of the box swallowed up the dime. Then he pressed down on the accelerator and the streetcar lurched forward.

The man eyed Terry suspiciously. "You're out awful late for a young fellow, aren't you?" he asked. "This here is the last car of the night. How far are you going?"

Terry thought fast. "To the end of the line," he said. "I just live past the end of the line."

"Near Jane Street?" the car man asked.

"Yeah. Jane Street. I live on Jane Street."

"What number?" persisted the man.

"Ahh . . . one-oh-four." Terry could almost hear

Eric squawking, "Liar, liar, ten feet higher!" Darn him. If he hadn't been such a blabbermouth Terry wouldn't have had to leave home before he had enough money for South America.

"How old are you, sonny?"

There were no other passengers, so Terry was a captive audience.

"Fourteen," he lied again. ("One lie leads to another," he heard Aunt Lottie say in his mind.)

"You're awful small for fourteen."

"I take after my dad. He was a short guy." Lie number four . . . his dad had been over six feet tall.

"What do you mean, was?"

"I mean is . . . he is tall . . . I mean short!" (There was Aunt Lottie's voice again: "Oh, what a tangled web we weave, when first we practice to deceive.")

Just then the driver's attention was taken with maneuvering the streetcar as it curved, with a loud screech of steel on steel, into the loop at Bloor and Jane Streets.

"This is it, kid. End of the line. I'm heading for the barns now."

Terry stepped down on the treadle, but the door didn't open. "How come you're out so late?" the driver persisted.

"Um . . . I had to stay with my grandma until my grandpa got home from work. He's on the night shift. My grandma's old and sick." He'd lost count of the lies by now.

"Do you mind telling me your name?"

Terry shifted from foot to foot. This driver was getting too darn nosy, and Terry wished he'd mind his own business. But he knew he had to answer if he wanted to get out the door. "My name's Joe Smith." The lies were getting easier and easier.

Slowly the driver pulled the handle that opened the door. "Goodnight, Joe Smith," he said.

"'Night!" Terry yelled as he jumped down the steps, ran across Bloor, and headed up Jane Street. He turned up his collar against the cold night air. At least it had stopped snowing, and the moon was out.

Suddenly Terry spotted another policeman, swinging his nightstick, and he darted into the nearest laneway.

His heart pounding, he pressed himself flat against a chain-link fence. The officer paused, glanced up the lane, then sauntered on by.

"Whew!" Terry whispered relaxing against the fence. Then all of a sudden something crashed into his back, sending him sprawling onto the frozen gravel. Terrified, the wind knocked out of him, he turned over, raised up on his elbows and found himself staring right into the gleaming green eyes of a big German shepherd. The dog was on its hind legs, barking furiously, its ears standing up like darts.

Suddenly the door to the house behind the fence flew open. "Hey, you, Queenie!" The silhouette of a man stood out sharply against the yellow light in the doorway. "What's all that racket about?" He stepped out onto the porch and peered into the semi-darkness. Terry froze. "Brrr!" shivered the man, slapping his arms. Then he yelled at the dog again. "Get back into your kennel before you wake up the whole neighbourhood." With that he jumped back inside the house and slammed the door.

The dog, its tail between its legs, slunk away towards a shed at the end of the yard.

Terry got up slowly and crept to the fence. His eyes had adjusted to the dark and he could see clearly by the moonlight. "Hey, Queenie!" he whispered in a wheedling voice. The dog turned and took a few uncertain steps towards him. Terry could hear a rumbling in her throat, but he noticed that her tail was wagging.

"Good girl, Queenie. Nice doggie. Come and see me." The dog came a little closer. The rumble had changed to a soft whine. Terry recognized the signs. When he had lived at home with his family their next door neighbours had had a big Labrador retriever that had acted just like that when he wanted to be friends.

Now Queenie's bushy tail was swishing around in excited circles. She gave a gleeful little yelp. "Shhh!" whispered Terry, glancing fearfully at the house. Then he remembered the chocolate bars in his pocket. He pulled one out, unwrapped it, and poked it through the fence. The dog took it neatly in her razor-sharp teeth, swallowed it in one gulp, and began licking his fingers.

That was all the invitation Terry needed. Sticking the toe of his boots between the chain links, he scaled the fence and dropped into the yard. Instantly the dog pounced on him and knocked him flat. For a split second he was petrified — until she began slathering his face with kisses.

"Nice girl!" he murmured as he wriggled out from under her big furry body and scrambled to his feet.

Gripping his sleeve between her teeth, she began dragging him towards the backyard shed. The door was ajar so she went in, turned around, and stuck out her nose. "Ruff!" she said.

Terry darted another anxious look at the house. The windows were dark now. He looked back at Queenie. Her eyes were glittering like emeralds; her whole body was quivering with excitement.

"Ruff!" she said invitingly.

Terry stepped inside the shed. He could smell oil and gasoline and musty old clothes. In the middle of the floor was a pile of rags.

Queenie began turning round and round in the heap of rags as if she were chasing her tail. Terry knew that she was making her bed. When it suited her, she flopped down and gazed up at him. "Woof!" she said.

Laughing softly, he dropped to his knees, threw his arms around her and buried his face in the thick ruff on her neck. They shared the second chocolate bar. Then Terry curled up in the curve of her furry body and, warmed by her winter coat, drifted off to sleep.

The last thing he remembered was her silky tongue licking the salt tears off his face.

Chapter 11

Freedom

That night Terry had a spectacular dream. A huge fire, a conflagration bigger than all the fires he'd ever seen rolled into one, engulfed Ossington Avenue. Every house from Bloor Street to College was swallowed in a torrent of orange flames, and he, Terry Dawson, with his intrepid dog, Queenie, saved every living soul. The last person he pulled out of the inferno was his Aunt Lottie. When she opened her eyes and saw who her rescuer was she threw her arms around his neck and cried, "My hero!" covering his face with kisses.

It was the kisses that woke him up. For a split second he didn't know where he was, then the silky tongue licking his cheeks made him remember.

"I gotta get outta here, Queenie!" he whispered.

Scrambling to his feet, Terry stretched to get the

kinks out of his muscles. Then he leaned down and patted his new friend between her ears. "Bye, girl," he said. "I'll be seeing you." The dog sat up anxiously on her haunches, so Terry pointed his finger at her and commanded, "Stay!"

Easing the shed door open, he peered up at the house. It was still in darkness. So he crept to the chain-link fence, climbed it easily, and was soon strolling nonchalantly down Jane Street in the grey morning light.

A streetcar was waiting at the loop so Terry unbuttoned his pocket and got another dime out of his money bag.

The streetcar door clunked open and the driver said, "You're up pretty early, aren't you, sonny?"

For an instant Terry thought it was the same driver. No, this guy was a lot younger. Streetcar men sure were nosy-parkers.

He decided to stick to his story. "I have to get to my grandma's before my grandpa goes to work." His dime clinked in the glass fare box and he asked for a transfer. Then he sauntered down the aisle and took a seat near the back.

Looking out the window, he saw a man going into a greasy-spoon restaurant. Hunger pangs began to gnaw at his stomach. His mouth watered for a steaming bowl of Red River Cereal. But in spite of his hunger he enjoyed the jiggly ride along Bloor Street. Storekeepers were throwing up their blinds and people were milling at the streetcar stops on their way to work.

Suddenly the driver hollered, "Next stop, Ossington!" and Terry remembered his dream. It had been so real he was afraid to look, so he crossed the aisle and stared out the opposite window. And there, leaning on the doorjamb of Fire Station 14, was Joe Hancock.

Terry jerked his eyes away, his heart pounding. Had Joe seen him? He didn't dare glance back. Now he had the awful feeling that everybody on the streetcar was looking at him. He fixed his gaze out the window and began reading the store signs. "Boulter's Butcher Shop . . . Homemade sausages and weiners." "Aikenhead's Hardware . . . Everything for the handyman." "Tamblyn's Drug Store." "The Fancy Floral Shoppe" . . . The Fancy Floral Shoppe!

Sliding down until his eyes were just level with the window sill, he retracted his head inside his collar like a turtle. His heart was doing nip-ups. What if Aunt Lottie had spotted him? He pinched back his sleeve and glanced at his watch. Seven-thirty. It was still too early for his aunt to be at work.

Just when he was sure everyone must be staring at him a woman got on the streetcar, dragging a small boy with a brown paper bag over his head. From under the bag came a loud wail of protest.

"Shut up!" hissed the woman.

But the boy managed to snatch the bag off and under it, wedged tight on his little head just level with his tear-filled eyes, was a white enamel chamber pot. The handle of the pot stuck out like an enormous extra ear.

The crowded streetcar erupted in a roar of laughter and the embarrassed woman, her face flaming red, jammed the paper bag back on her son's head.

Sure that nobody was noticing him, Terry pulled the alley-bag out of his pocket by its string and began counting his money. Thirteen dollars and twenty cents. How far could he travel, he wondered, on thirteen dollars and twenty cents? He would have to go down to the bus terminal on Bay to find out. But first he decided to go downtown to see the Christmas decorations.

Chapter 12

Memories

It was too early for Simpson's and Eaton's to be open but people were already scurrying into Woolworth's. Terry followed the crowd. All the stools at the lunch counter were full so he bought himself a doughnut and took it along to Eaton's. Huddled in the doorway of the big department store, he munched on the warm doughnut.

At last a man in an Eaton uniform appeared inside and unlocked the revolving doors.

Shivering with the cold now, Terry gave the carousel of doors a hard push. But they were so heavy they stopped halfway and he got trapped in the middle. Panicky, he shoved with all his might. At the same time someone pushed on the door behind him. It caught him in the back and sent him sprawling into the store.

The man in uniform looked down on him suspiciously. Terry picked himself up, brushed himself off, and walked away trying not to seem in a hurry. As he passed the bronze statue of Timothy Eaton sitting high up on its pedestal, he remembered that his mother always rubbed the shiny toe of the statue for good luck. He took off his mitt and brushed it lightly, wondering when his mother had touched it last.

As soon as he was out of sight of the Eaton man Terry made a beeline for the washrooms in the basement. He had to go so badly he thought he'd burst. Afterwards, his stomach easing with relief, he took the express elevator up to Toyland.

Santa Claus was just getting settled on his throne in his crystal palace. A girl dressed like an elf was filling a basket with Christmas candies. She glanced up, flashed him a dazzling smile, and tossed him a candy cane. He caught it and laughed. Santa stroked his wavy white beard and winked. Terry winked back. Stripping off the cellophane he sucked gratefully on the pointed end of the candy cane.

Just then the first visitor arrived: a small boy and his mother. When the little fellow spotted Santa he let out a whoop, dropped his mother's hand, and raced up the wooden ramp. Placing his chubby hands on the red velvet knees he stared up at his hero and began reciting his Christmas list.

A pain stabbed Terry's heart. "Albert!" The name came out of his mouth before he could stop it. He knew the kid wasn't Albert. He didn't look the least bit like Albert. Besides, his brother was dead. Why had he said that?

The boy's mother stared at him curiously. Embarrassed, Terry hurried away and jumped on the escalator. Riding down from floor to floor, he remembered his own Christmas lists: it was always bicycles, wagons, and fire trucks. He remembered his last toy fire truck: it had extension ladders, bells, sirens, and a hose with a pumper that shot out real water. His mother had made him keep it in the cellar so he wouldn't mess up the kitchen floor. He smiled at the memory, then frowned, wondering where his fire truck was today. When he had gone to the first foster home he had left his toys behind.

He stepped off the escalator at Boys' Wear and was instantly pounced upon by an idle saleslady. "Aren't you supposed to be in school?" she inquired sharply.

Sheesh, Terry thought, another nosy grown-up. "My mother sent me to buy a new winter coat." The lie rolled easily off his tongue.

The tall, spare woman pulled in her pointed chin and surveyed him over her bifocals. She reminded him of his Aunt Lottie. "And not a minute too soon if you ask me," she remarked sourly.

Terry made a face at her back as she went towards the coat rack. "Who asked you, you old biddy," he muttered.

She turned suddenly, holding out a plaid lumberjacket.

"Did you say something?" she snapped.

"Nope," answered Terry innocently.

"Then try this on for size. It's fleece-lined. Just the thing for this cold weather."

"Uhh . . . " Terry backed off. "How much?"

"It's a pre-Christmas special. Regularly $25.98, but I can let you have it for $15.98. I'm sure your mother wouldn't want you to pass up such a bargain."

"My mom told me to take my time," Terry hedged.

Just then the telephone on the counter rang. "Stay right where you are. Don't move a muscle. I'll be right back," commanded the sergeant-major of a saleslady.

The minute her back was turned Terry made his getaway. Still, no matter where he went he had the eerie feeling that people were watching him, so he kept on the move, wandering from floor to floor.

Back on the main floor, Terry glanced at his

watch again. It read nine o'clock, but his grumbling stomach told him it must be much later than that. He shook his wrist and pressed the watch to his ear. He had forgotten to wind it. He looked around for a clock, then got up the nerve to ask a floorwalker for the time.

The floorwalker pulled his pocket-watch out by its chain and snapped it open. "It's eleven o'clock on the dot. Shouldn't you be in school?"

Muttering a disgusted, "Geez!" Terry headed straight for the revolving doors. Once outside he stopped to set and wind his watch. It wasn't nearly lunchtime but he was starving. Then his eyes brightened. "I think I'll go where Mom used to take Albert and me. Across Yonge Street to the Honey Dew."

It had started to snow again. On the corner the Salvation Army Band was lustily playing "Good King Wenceslas," and Terry began to feel Christmassy in spite of himself.

Remembering that his mother had always given to what she called "a worthy cause," he dug into his money bag and came up with a fifty-cent piece. He hesitated, the big silver coin clutched tightly in his palm, and thought of his mother saying, "Do what your heart tells you to, Terry."

The money clanked among the smaller coins in

the kettle. "God bless you, son. And Merry Christmas!" the Army man said, and he didn't even ask Terry why he wasn't in school.

"You're welcome, and same to you!" Terry laughed.

Inside the restaurant he spent another quarter on a glistening red-hot and a sparkling orange Honey Dew. Boy, it was a swell feeling to be independent. But his money was going fast. "Only got $12.25 left," he calculated as he squeezed a winding yellow path of mustard on his hot dog.

How could he earn some more money, he wondered. Maybe he could work here in the Honey Dew and get free dogs and dews every day. Or maybe he could be a bellhop in the Royal York Hotel and get a free room every night.

He felt so much better after eating that he got up the nerve to go up to the counter and ask a lady with Honey Dew sewn on her pocket if there were any jobs to be had.

"How old are you, sonny?" she asked suspiciously.

"I'm fourteen," he lied.

"In a pig's eye!" she snorted and walked away. Red with embarrassment, he stomped out of the restaurant.

If only he was taller and had a beard. He took

off his mitt and scratched his chin. Darn! Not even peach fuzz. Oh, well, there was still one consolation: he wouldn't have to go to school any more. But his mom and dad would be disappointed if they knew. They had always told him if he stayed in school he could be anything he wanted to be. His Aunt Betty would be disappointed too, and she would know because she was still alive. He sighed and tried not to think about it.

On Queen Street a policeman wearing white gloves was directing traffic between Eaton's and Simpson's. Terry crossed with the crowd and stopped to gaze at the animated winter scene in Simpson's corner window. Little bears and elves and pixies twirled in circles on a miniature ice-rink. He remembered the last time he had peered in that window. With Albert. Albert had flattened his little pug nose against the cold glass and squealed with delight. A lump rose in Terry's throat and he turned quickly away.

Chapter 13

In the News

Simpson's doors revolved with a steady stream of shoppers. Terry let himself be swept inside. Signs of the holiday season were everywhere. Terry rode the escalators, gazing up at the glittering garlands, red and green streamers, and shiny aluminum trees. They had always had a real tree at their house. His dad had insisted on it. They used to go way out to a farmer's field in Agincourt and cut their own spruce tree.

He jumped off the escalator in the furniture department to see what was new in television sets. A big sharp black-and-white screen showed the noon news. A wide red ribbon across one corner of the set read: "21" Sylvania, $599.99." Terry whistled at the price. The old ten-inch set at the house on Ossington was always going on the blink. Sometimes Terry could fix it himself, taking the tubes out to check on the tube-testing machine at the smoke shop. Even so, they didn't watch it much. Aunt Lottie always worried about wearing out the picture-tube. But every day at lunchtime, when Aunt Lottie wasn't home, Aunt Betty would turn on "Search for Tomorrow."

As soon as he got rich, he'd order up the biggest television he could find and have it delivered to Aunt Betty with a note that read: "Guess who?" She'd know. He'd buy himself one too. Then he'd never have to miss his favourite programs, "Dragnet" and "The Rifleman" and that great new western, "Gunsmoke." And he'd leave it on all day and all night and when the picture-tube burned out he'd just laugh and order up another.

Suddenly his daydream was interrupted by the words flashing across the giant screen: "NEWS BULLETIN!" Then the portrait of a family filled the screen. *His family!* There, large as life, were his mother and father and Albert. The camera zoomed in on one of the faces. "Have you seen this boy?" said the announcer. "He is 13-year-old Terence Dawson. He has dark curly hair," Terry yanked his toque down to his eyebrows, "and large brown eyes." Terry narrowed his eyes to slits. "Terence is wearing a lightweight plaid windbreaker and a red knitted toque." Terry snatched the toque off his head and stuffed it up the front of his windbreaker. "He has been missing from his Ossington Avenue home since late last night. Anyone having information concerning his whereabouts is asked to contact their local police department." At last the picture faded out, to be replaced by an accident scene.

Terry's first instinct was to bolt, but he was afraid that would attract attention. So he stayed rooted to the spot, not daring to look in any direction. He retracted his head like a turtle. What should he do? Where could he go? If only Frankie Weir were with him. Even Eric would be better than being alone. Well, maybe not. Besides being a traitor, he was such a scaredy-cat he would have run bawling home hours ago.

Joe Hancock was his friend, but Terry knew that if he phoned the firefighter, Joe would try to persuade him to go home.

Squinting through his thick black eyelashes, he saw that the crowd around the set was now completely engrossed in a Christmas show. No one seemed the least bit interested in a missing boy.

Cautiously he began threading his way through the maze of dank winter coats and fur-trimmed boots like his mother used to wear: high-heeled, with curly grey fur on black velvet. Squeezing onto the nearest elevator he rode down to the main floor. Then he slipped out the Yonge Street doors and crossed with the lights to wait at the northbound streetcar stop.

The temperature had dropped below zero and the wind blew right through his skimpy jacket and two sweaters. If only he could have afforded that fleece-lined lumberjacket. He put his toque back on, pulled the knitted band down to his eyebrows, and folded his thumbs inside his woollen mitts.

Stomping around to keep warm, head down, his mind a jumble of worries, he failed to notice that a gang of big boys had surrounded him like a pack of wolves. Before he had a chance to run, hands grabbed him from behind, pinning his arms to his sides. The boy in front of him jerked his chin up and forced him to look into his menacing black eyes.

"You got any money, kid?" he snarled.

"No!" Terry's voice choked with fear.

"Search the little twerp!" commanded the gang's leader, tightening his grip on Terry's collar.

There were five or six boys in the pack and they began tearing at his pockets. One tried to pry his wristwatch over his mittened fist. *The watch his parents had given him!* Fear gave way to fury and he began kicking and screaming with all his might.

Far outnumbered, Terry was losing badly when

a huge woman swinging a giant handbag ploughed into their midst. *Wham! Bam! Thump!* She sent them flying in all directions.

"Shame on you, you great ugly bullies! Picking on a boy half your size!" she bellowed.

Screaming in pain and holding onto their heads, they ran away, swearing at the top of their lungs.

The woman turned to Terry and said, "Are you alright, love?"

"Yes, thank you," breathed Terry, loosening his collar.

Then the woman reached into her handbag and pulled out an old-fashioned flat-iron. "Good thing I picked this up at the rummage sale this afternoon," she chortled. "Sure came in handy. Now here comes a streetcar. Have you got a ticket? Good . . . then away you go home, honey, before you get yourself hurt."

Waving at her through the streetcar window, he noticed through his tears how much she looked like Aunt Lottie.

He darted into a seat as a man got up. No sooner had he collapsed into it when the driver hollered, "Hey, you, kid. Come back here!"

Terry froze and everybody turned to stare at him. This time he knew the jig was up. On trembling legs he made his way back to the front of the car. "Ten cents," the carman said.

"Oh, sorry, sir." Terry dropped a dime into the box and remembered to ask for a transfer, then clung to the steel post near the door.

On the Bloor line he was lucky enough to get a seat again. The car was crowded with workers going home for supper and Terry felt very vulnerable. He scrunched down and stared out the snow-matted window into the passing darkness. After what seemed like hours, he got off at the end of the line. Jane Street.

The second he set foot on the sidewalk the tantalizing aroma of vinegar and chips wafted by his nose. He followed the delicious smell, his mouth watering, into the open door of the steamy little shop.

There were no seats left at the white enamel tables or the cosy side booths so he took his place at the end of the line. At last it was his turn.

"One order of fish and chips to go," he said, the money ready in his hand.

The man behind the counter, scooped the chips into an oblong box and, using tongs, placed a golden puff of fish on top. "You want salt and vinegar, son?" he asked, wiping his hands on his aproned stomach.

"Yes, please," answered Terry. He was almost drooling as he watched the food being generously doused with salt and vinegar. Then the man began to wrap the overflowing box in newspapers. The first fold of the paper cut right across a headline: *MISSING BOY!* Slowly the hot grease spread over a blurry picture of himself! His hand shook so badly he almost dropped the money.

"Are you cold, son?" the man asked kindly.

"No, sir. I mean, yes, sir," mumbled Terry.

"Well, this ought to warm you up!" He handed Terry the hot, greasy package and turned to his next customer.

Clutching the warm parcel against his chest, his heart in his mouth, Terry lowered his head and made for the door.

Safely out on the street again, under cover of a curtain of snow and darkness, Terry hurried towards Jane Street. He tore open one end of the package and ate as he went. The wonderful taste and aroma comforted him.

* * *

Queenie was right there waiting for him behind the chain link fence. She didn't make a sound but her bushy tail whirled like a windmill.

"Good girl, Queenie," Terry whispered. Instinctively they both looked towards the house. The kitchen blind was drawn but shadows could be seen moving about the lighted room.

Tucking the parcel inside his windbreaker, Terry scaled the fence and followed Queenie to her backyard shed.

There was still food in her dog dish and her water bowl was half full. With any luck, her owner wouldn't be coming out again tonight.

Terry sat cross-legged on the pile of rags. Queenie hunkered down beside him and they shared the feast together.

"You know what, Queen?" Terry whispered as he fed her a crispy chunk of fish. "You're about the best friend a guy ever had."

She pressed closer and licked the grease off his face with her silky pink tongue. "Ruff!" she replied in a dog whisper.

When they were finished eating they curled up together and once again Terry fell fast asleep in the warm protection of his new friend's furry body.

Again he dreamt about his aunts. This time Aunt Betty was crying hysterically and Aunt Lottie was trying to comfort her. Terry was just about to throw his arms around Aunt Betty and tell her that everything was okay when the shrill wail of a fire siren shattered his dream.

Chapter 14

Caught in the Act

A red glow, like a summer sunset, streaked through a crack in the shed wall.

Terry leapt to his feet and pressed one eye against the crack. "It's a fire, Queenie," he whispered, "and it's real close. I gotta go. You stay here."

Breathless with anticipation, he was the first to arrive at the scene. Orange flames were shooting out a store's front window and licking up the flat surface of the white frame building. Enticed, as always, by the fire's magnetic force, Terry crept closer and closer until he could feel the intense heat radiating upon his face.

Suddenly, with a tremendous crash, a basement window exploded. Instantly Terry was engulfed in a rolling black cloud. Reeling back, he clutched at his throat, coughing and choking and gasping for air.

The last thing he remembered were screaming sirens and flashing lights and the deafening roar of the fire. Then he felt himself spinning and falling into a deep black abyss.

* * *

Aunt Betty's worried face floated in and out of focus.

His eyelids were so heavy that he could hardly lift them up. He tried to speak but his tongue felt thick as wool. Then, Aunt Lottie's voice, sharp as a knife, cut through his fuzzy thoughts. "Wake up, Terence!" she commanded.

He blinked hard and his singed eyelashes rustled like dried leaves.

He recognized both aunts, but he couldn't figure out where he was. Why were the walls stark white and his bed so high up off the floor? And who was the stranger hovering over him, with the thick black beard and earphones around his neck?

"Who are you?" Terry didn't recognize the voice croaking from his dry throat.

The stranger smiled and said something through the black bush that sounded like, "Dr. Frankenstein."

"Frankenstein!" Terry shrank back in terror against the flat pillow.

Quickly Aunt Betty reached out and squeezed his hand. "Not Frankenstein, Terry, Frankline. This is Dr. Frankline."

Nudging her sister aside impatiently, Aunt Lottie loomed over him. "You owe your life to Dr. Frankline, young man," she said reproachfully.

"I'm sorry," Terry apologized. "I didn't mean anything."

"The boy is not himself, Miss Dawson," reproved the doctor. Aunt Lottie said, "Hmph!" and stepped back. Then Dr. Frankline spoke to Terry.

"I'm going to give you something to help you sleep now, son. We'll talk later."

* * *

"Are you awake, boy?" The loud male voice made Terry jerk into consciousness. His dark eyes sprang open and looked directly into the steely gaze of a man in uniform. A police uniform.

"Do you feel up to answering a few questions?" asked the policeman, not unkindly.

"I guess so," Terry said. But he was confused. What could he know that the police would be interested in?

"Don't be afraid, Terry. Just tell the truth." Dr. Frankline stood beside him, his fingers pressing the inside of Terry's thin wrist. He nodded towards the policeman.

"I'm Constable Stephens," began the lawman. "Now, what can you tell me about the Jane Street fire?"

"Nothing."

"Do you know how it got started?"

"No."

"Where were you when you first spotted it?"

"In a shed."

A sudden glance at Aunt Lottie made him decide in a split second not to mention Queenie.

"Now, Terry." The policeman regarded him sternly. "I'm going to ask you a question straight from the shoulder. And I want a straight answer. Understand?"

"Yes, sir." Terry was getting scared.

"Did you set fire to that building?"

"*Me! Start a fire!?*" Terry shot bolt upright and the room whirled around him. "I don't start fires. I stop them. You can ask Joe Hancock if you don't believe me. He's a firefighter and he's my friend and he knows."

Exhausted by his outburst, Terry fell back on the pillow. Brusquely the doctor ordered everybody out of the room. Terry felt a sharp tweak in his arm and he fell asleep almost instantly.

The next time he woke only his aunts were there.

"How did you find me?" he asked Aunt Betty.

"We couldn't sleep a wink after you disappeared," she said. "We sat by the phone waiting for it to ring. Then last night on the eleven o'clock news they showed the fire on Jane Street and we saw someone being carried away on a stretcher. The stretcher passed right by the news camera and there was a close-up of the victim's face. And it was you!"

"You're kidding!" cried Terry

"If you mean joking, no we are not!" snapped Aunt Lottie. "The sight of you gave us a terrible turn."

"You mean I was really on television?" Terry grinned.

"Yes, you were. And we thought you were dead." Aunt Betty's pale blue eyes filled with tears.

"I'm awful sorry I scared you, Aunt Betty." He reached for her hand. "I'm sorry for everything, Aunt Lottie."

"Well, you'll be a lot sorrier before this affair is over." Aunt Lottie rose abruptly from the visitor's chair and began tugging on her gloves. "You see, the Fire Chief suspects arson and he has ordered a full investigation into this fire. And who do you think their prime suspect is?"

"Who?" Terry asked.

"Who indeed!" snorted Aunt Lottie. "Who rushes to every fire? Who always arrives before the fire department? And who runs away from a perfectly good home for no better reason than to chase fire trucks? Who indeed!"

"I'm sure Terry can explain," murmured Aunt Betty. She looked at her nephew pleadingly. "Won't you tell us where you've been these last two dreadful days and nights, Terry? And why did you run away?" Now the tears spilled down her cheeks. "You must have known we'd be worried sick about you."

Seeing the pain he'd caused his favourite aunt, Terry was suddenly overcome with remorse.

"I'm sorry! I'm sorry!" he cried, throwing up his arm to hide the flood of tears.

"Well, sorry you might be." Aunt Lottie's voice shook with emotion. "But it's not enough this time. And if I have my way you'll be sent where you belong."

Terry's folded arms thumped down on his chest. His wet face was sheet white and his eyes grew so big and dark that the pupils seemed to merge with the iris.

"Where?" he demanded.

Charlotte Dawson couldn't meet her nephew's accusing stare so she fixed her gaze somewhere above his head and answered in a harsh whisper,

"To the Boys' Correctional Centre, that's where."

Upon hearing these awful words Elizabeth Dawson drew herself up to her full height of five feet two inches. Her pale eyes had suddenly caught fire.

"Over my dead body!" she cried.

Chapter 15

House Arrest

Terry was placed under house arrest. He was only allowed out of the house to attend school. His orders were to go straight there and straight back again.

Joe Hancock came by the minute he got word. Aunt Lottie answered the doorbell.

"Good evening, ma'am." Joe removed his hat politely. "I've come to see Terry."

"Terence is not allowed visitors." Charlotte Dawson replied curtly, and she began to shut the door in his face.

Joe spread a big hand on the door and held it firmly open. "I don't think you understand. I'm the boy's friend and I've come to see if there is anything I can do to help."

"There's nothing anyone can do," she answered coldly.

As she pushed on the door, Elizabeth Dawson came from the kitchen, wiping her hands on her apron. Two red patches burned on her round cheeks. "How dare you say that without consulting me, Charlotte?" she demanded. Pushing past her sister she spoke to the tall stranger still standing outside the door. "Any friend of Terry's is a friend of mine. Won't you come in?"

Joe stepped inside and Aunt Betty called up the stairwell, "Terry, you have a visitor!"

Terry had been hanging over the banister straining his ears, but he hadn't quite recognized the man's voice.

"I don't want to see nobody!" he yelled back.

"Then I guess I'm just wasting my time!" Joe shouted.

Instantly Terry came flying down the stairs.

"Joe! Joe!" he cried, running straight into the big fireman's arms. "I knew you'd come. Aunt Betty . . . Aunt Lottie . . . this here's Firefighter Joe Hancock and he knows I'm innocent. Did you talk to the fire chief yet, Joe? Did you tell him I'm not the firebug?"

"Now hold on a minute." Joe kept his arm protectively around Terry's shoulders. "Is there somewhere we can talk?" he asked Aunt Betty.

"Certainly. Come into the living room." Ignoring

her sister's baleful stare she led the way through the french doors.

"You and Terry sit there." She pointed with a pudgy finger to the chesterfield. They sat down and Aunt Lottie was just about to sit opposite them on the matching chair when Aunt Betty caught her by the arm and tugged her to her feet.

"Come along, Charlotte. We have other things to do."

Dumbfounded by her younger sister's sudden assertiveness, Charlotte allowed herself to be led from the room.

Joe threw one long arm across the back of the chesterfield behind Terry's head. With his free hand he stroked his brown moustache thoughtfully. "I believe you when you say you had nothing to do with the Jane Street fire, Terry. Or any other fire for that matter. And I'll certainly speak on your behalf. But what we need is proof. And we haven't got it."

Terry's unruly black curls drooped over his forehead as he stared dejectedly at the floor.

"If Queenie could talk, I'd have proof," he said.

"Can you tell me about Queenie?" Joe asked.

"Only if you promise not to tell my aunts."

"Why not?"

"Because Aunt Lottie would be mad at me for sleeping with a dog."

Joe couldn't help but laugh. "I promise," he said.

So Terry told him how he'd spent those two cold nights.

"And the dog's owner never saw you?"

"Nope."

"Did anyone see you?"

"The streetcar drivers. But they didn't know where I was going."

Joe asked more questions and Terry answered them all truthfully.

"Well, son." Joe ruffled Terry's hair reassuringly as he got up to leave. "Stay calm and keep a stiff upper lip. I'll see what I can do."

* * *

The first day back at school was hard. The news of Terry's escapades had spread like wildfire and kids he'd never even spoken to before flocked around him like seagulls; some of the others avoided him like the plague.

The school principal watched him like a hawk, as if he expected him to burn the school down any minute. And Mr. Snarr ostracized him completely, acting as if Terry wasn't even in the classroom.

After school that day Eric raced on his bike to catch up to Terry, his ears flapping in the wind. "Want to be buddies again?" he asked hopefully.

Buddies? Terry thought. When had they ever

been buddies? In answer, he stood up on the pedals and put on a burst of speed. Eric pedalled furiously to catch up to him.

"You can trust me, Terry, honest. I learnt my lesson. I'll never tell a grownup another secret as long as I live. Geez, you can't even trust your own mother."

You can't trust your own mother? Terry frowned at the thought. If his mother was here, would she believe in him? Yes, she would. He knew she would. She would never let him down. But you couldn't count on aunts. Aunt Lottie was purposely ignoring him, just like Snarkey Snarr. And Aunt Betty . . . well, she had stuck up for him against Aunt Lottie and he knew that was hard for her to do. But she wasn't as much fun as she used to be.

"Okay," he said to Eric. He really needed a friend right now.

But the minute they stopped in front of Eric's house the door flew open and Mrs. Thurston came charging out onto the veranda waving a wooden spoon.

"I thought I told you to stay away from him!" she shrieked, jabbing the handle of the spoon in Terry's direction like a spear. "He's got a bad reputation and I don't want you tarred with the same brush. Birds of a feather flock together, you know! That's what people will say. Now get in here before I skin you alive."

Dropping his bike like a hot potato, Eric leapt up the steps. As he darted past her, his mother cracked him over the head with the bowl of the spoon and slammed the door behind them.

Terry stood astride his bike, seething with anger. It boiled up inside him like a volcano. He wanted to bash down the door and yell swear words at Mrs. Thurston at the top of his lungs. Then he remembered Joe's advice to stay cool. "So much for buddies," he shrugged.

He rode home slowly, propped his bike against the porch, and went in.

Aunt Betty turned from the counter where she was making a lemon cake out of Kate Aitken's cookbook. Blowing a wisp of fluffy fair hair out of her troubled blue eyes, she asked, "How was school today, Terry?"

"Okay," he muttered, and went straight upstairs.

At the supper table the three of them sat in total silence. Aunt Lottie had been tight-lipped ever since her sister had usurped her authority. Terry didn't really mind, but he missed Aunt Betty's cheerful chatter.

Nights were the worst. There was nothing to do

but homework, and even on the weekends he wasn't allowed to watch television. That was a big part of his punishment. He hated missing Ed Sullivan on Sunday nights.

Aunt Lottie had even punished herself and Aunt Betty by not watching the Christmas specials. Terry missed seeing "Bing Crosby's Family Christmas" and Perry Como, and especially "A Christmas Carol."

Christmas day came and went and the only concession Aunt Lottie made for the holiday was a turkey dinner and a dark fruit cake from Hunt's Bakery. Otherwise the day was as dreary as any other.

And the Fire Department's investigation seemed as if it was going to drag on forever.

Chapter 16

Flying the Coop

One January night, Terry lay in bed pondering his fate. "I'm a prisoner, anyway," he thought to himself, "so why not escape again?" The idea made him spring to life.

He couldn't go to South America, of course. He knew that dream would have to wait a few years. But he *could* go as far as Jane Street.

He had flown the coop before — that was no problem. And this time he was better prepared. Lately, without really knowing why, he had been bringing his outdoor clothes up to his room instead of hanging them in the back porch or down in the cellar.

Easing himself out of bed, he dressed quietly and counted the loose change in his pocket. Two quarters, two dimes and a nickel. While his aunts had been watching Lawrence Welk and his champagne music on television, Terry had raided the cracked sugar bowl where Aunt Betty kept change to pay the paper-boy. Terry didn't consider it stealing because Aunt Lottie had confiscated what was left of his money. Confiscating sure seemed a lot like stealing to him, so he figured the sugar bowl was fair game.

Next he found a scrap of paper, scribbled a note on it, and tucked it into his windbreaker pocket. Then he turned off the green bottle lamp, fell back on his pillow, clasped his hands behind his head, and waited for the night noises that would tell him the house was asleep.

Pretty soon he heard the rumble of the self-feeding furnace as it gobbled up the coal, and the loud, erratic snoring coming through the register from Aunt Lottie's room.

Terry rose carefully so the bedsprings wouldn't squeak, eased the casement window open, slid over the sill, eased the window almost shut, and began the precarious climb down the television tower.

The aerial jiggled and swayed overhead and the steel bars of the tower made cracking noises as he descended it like a ladder to the ground.

The minute he landed he made a beeline for Bloor Street and boarded a westbound streetcar. As bad luck would have it, he met up with the same driver.

"Hello there, Joe Smith," grinned the car man amiably as he flicked the lever on the fare box that swallowed up Terry's dime. "Been to visit your granny again, I see."

"Yep." Terry smiled with relief. Obviously the driver hadn't recognized him from the blurry picture in the paper, and he really believed that his name was Joe Smith.

"She sure is a lucky lady to have a grandson like you. You're a good lad," continued the man.

"Thanks!" Terry freely accepted the compliment. "If I did have a grandma," he reasoned, "I *would* be good to her."

He got off at the end of the line and again followed his nose into the crowded fish-and-chip shop. A woman with a red face and frowzy grey hair was busy shaking a basket of golden fries over the boiling oil. He got into line.

Terry couldn't afford fish this time, but with the hot chips wrapped in newspapers and tucked inside his jacket he headed straight for Jane Street.

Queenie was waiting behind the chain-link fence just as if she had known he was coming. He wondered if dogs had a special gift of telepathy.

Terry settled down cross-legged on the bed of

rags and breathed in the clean scent of Sunlight soap. Queenie's owner must have just done the wash. Queenie hunkered down beside him. Piece by piece, Terry shared the crunchy chips with his best friend, and all his troubles, too. They seemed to come pouring out of him, and every time he paused to chew or take a breath Queenie nuzzled him with her wet nose. "Woof," she said, as if begging him to continue. She sure was a good listener. Two hours passed like two minutes.

When at last he got up to leave, Queenie whined beseechingly.

"I'm sorry, Queenie, but I gotta go. If I get caught I'll end up in the clink for sure." He leaned down and stroked the frown on her forehead and gently pulled her ears. "But don't worry. I'll be back. You stay, that's a good girl."

In the dim light seeping through the cracks of the shed wall, her starry eyes glistened with uncanny understanding.

* * *

Emerging stealthily from the laneway, Terry glanced furtively up and down Jane Street. No one was in sight. He fished the note out of his pocket and re-read it by the yellow light of the street lamp. "If you ever need anybody to mind Queenie you only have to let me know," the note said. Under the message he had printed his name and address. He didn't dare give his phone number in case Aunt Lottie might answer.

Sneaking up onto the dark veranda of Queenie's owner's house, he slipped the note noiselessly into the letter box. Then he crept back down the wooden steps and, once safely on the sidewalk, he took off like a shot.

Luck was with him the rest of the way. He didn't run into any patrolling policemen and the streetcar driver was a perfect stranger who didn't even bother to say hello.

Cautiously Terry climbed back up the television tower, pausing with his heart in his mouth every time it scraped against the bricks. The casement window opened smoothly on its steel track. Hefting himself over the sill, he drew the window shut behind him.

Shivering in the cold room, he pulled on his fleecy polo pyjamas and crept gratefully under the feather comforter that had been his one and only Christmas present from his aunts.

Gradually the bed warmed up and he began to feel terrific. What a great night it had been! What a swell friend Queenie was. Maybe he'd visit her every night . . .

Just as he was dozing off, a memory hit him like

a thunderbolt. On the black wrought-iron letter-box of Queenie's owner's house, painted in white, had been the number 104 — the exact same address he had blurted out to that first streetcar driver. Was it just a weird co-incidence? Or was it some kind of omen? He might never know what had led him to Queenie's house, but he was sure grateful.

Chapter 17

Exoneration

One day near the end of the third week of his sentence Terry came home in a bad mood. Old Snarkey Snarr had been picking on him again and Eric was still avoiding him. But that was okay, Terry figured, because he was sick of Eric anyway. Stupid snivelling snitch, he thought balefully.

Aunt Betty was just lighting up her last cigarette of the day. With a little puff she blew out the match and let thin trails of smoke filter through her button nose. The cigarette bobbing on her lower lip, she began setting the table. A bright red ash fell onto the plastic cloth and instantly ignited. Terry snuffed it out with his thumb.

"Ouch!" he cried, sucking at the burn. "Don't you know that most house fires are caused by careless smoking?" he snapped crankily.

Aunt Betty stopped what she was doing, un-stuck the newly lit cigarette with the tip of her tongue, and dunked it with a sizzle into a basin of water in the sink. Then she got the package of Exports from behind the bread tin and dropped it, along with the soggy cigarette, into the garbage can.

"What did you do that for?" asked Terry.

"Because I know you're right," she said.

* * *

Aunt Lottie was in a foul mood when she came home. Apparently the flowers she had prepared for a big wedding had frozen on the way to the church and the bride's parents were refusing to pay. "As if I can be held responsible for a change in the weather," she fumed. "Fools! The world is full of fools!"

"Perhaps you could sue," suggested Aunt Betty.

"Don't talk nonsense, Elizabeth. It costs more to sue than it's worth. If you have nothing intelligent to say, say nothing at all."

Insulted by her sister's remark, Aunt Betty pursed her pink lips in a tight bow and clattered the rest of the cutlery onto the table. The meal was eaten in stony silence. Terry picked all the hated peas out of his beef stew and built a wall along the edge of his plate, cementing it together with mashed potatoes. Ordinarily this would have brought on a lecture by Aunt Lottie about all the starving children of the world who would be glad to eat his peas. But today neither one of his aunts paid the slightest attention to what he was doing. Somehow, Terry thought, he would have preferred the lecture.

Another miserable evening stretched out gloomily ahead of them. Terry felt his spirits sinking to an all-time low. Was he really going to have to spend the rest of his natural life penned up in this prison with two warden aunts?

His gloomy thoughts were interrupted by the harsh jangle of the doorbell. Glad of the distraction, Terry leapt to answer it, hoping it was Joe. But it wasn't. Instead, two tall, intimidating strangers filled the doorway.

"Is this the Dawson household?" one man asked.

"Yeah." Terry looked up into the long, serious face apprehensively. Who are these guys? he wondered.

"We'd like to speak to Miss Dawson," the other man said in a deep voice.

"Which one?"

At that precise moment Aunt Lottie appeared in the hall doorway and nudged her nephew aside with her sharp hipbone. "I am Miss Charlotte Dawson," she announced importantly. "What can I do for you gentlemen?"

"Are you the guardian of Master Terence Dawson?"

"I am."

Terry felt his stomach muscles tighten. Then Aunt Betty came up behind him and placed her hands protectively on his shoulders. "My name is Elizabeth Dawson," she declared. "And I, too, am Terry's guardian."

"Then let me introduce myself and my partner. I am Investigator Hunter of the Fire Department. And this is Detective Alberto of the Metropolitan Police." The plainclothes policeman flipped open a leather folder and Terry caught the flash of a silver badge. His apprehension grew. "May we come in?"

"Certainly!" said Aunt Lottie and she led them, like a parade, into the living room. Aunt Betty kept her hands firmly planted on Terry's shoulders.

The two men removed their dark fedoras and sat on the edge of the chesterfield.

Placing his hat on one knee, the fire investigator looked directly at Terry. "Are you the boy in question?" he asked.

Before Terry could answer, Aunt Lottie butted in. "Yes, this is Terence Dawson. What has he done now?"

Investigator Hunter frowned at her question. "I'd prefer the boy speak for himself." He scrutinized Terry, who quickly folded his burnt thumb inside his fist.

Aunt Lottie huffed and snapped her mouth shut.

Terry twisted his shoulders away from Aunt Betty and stood alone on the carpet. "My name is Terence Wendell Dawson, but my friends call me Terry. The Wendell comes from my mother's side. I'm nearly thirteen and I'm in grade eight and I haven't done a thing. Is there anything else you want to know?" In spite of his growing fear, a touch of defiance crept into his voice.

"Well, Terence," the investigator's face remained solemn, "the inquiry into the Jane Street fire has finally been completed and we have found no evidence to link you with the incident."

Terry let out a whoop of triumph. "You mean I'm free?" Joe must have put in a good word for him. It sure helped to have friends in high places! Suddenly he turned on his grim-faced Aunt Lottie. "See! I told you I was innocent but you wouldn't believe me. I told you both!" he yelled.

"Stop right there!" Detective Alberto raised his hand to silence Terry's outburst. "You're not in the clear yet, young man. Not by a long shot. For lack of evidence we can't charge you, so you are no longer under house arrest. But you are under strict orders to stay away from all fire scenes and fire stations until further notice. Do you read me?"

"Well, that's not fair!" Terry's black eyes were shooting sparks. "I didn't do anything wrong so I should be able to go wherever I like. It's a free country, you know."

His insolence unsnapped Aunt Lottie's jaw with a clack. "Be quiet, you ungrateful boy. You should consider yourself lucky to get off so lightly."

The two officials rose to leave and Terry heard his Aunt Lottie assuring them, as she escorted them to the door, that their orders would be carried out to the letter.

Terry was still fuming when Aunt Lottie returned to the living room. Her mouth was set in a hard, uncompromising line.

"No, for you, it is not a free country because you have not yet been exonerated. You simply haven't been charged. There's a world of difference. You could still be found guilty."

"You'd like that, wouldn't you?" Terry's rage at life's unfairness had made him lose all fear. "You'd like to see me thrown in jail. Then you'd be rid of me for good!"

Suddenly Aunt Lottie's face turned from white to red. "Go to bed this instant!" she commanded.

"Get out of my sight!"

"Oh, Terry, Terry!" Aunt Betty's pitiful cry followed him as he ran up the two flights of stairs. He slammed the attic door, threw himself on the bed and gave himself up to tears of rage.

Scrubbing at his eyes with tight fists, he muttered angrily. "Who does she think she is, sending me to bed like a two-year-old. I'm thirteen and I can do what I like."

After sneaking in and out of the house six times without being caught, he felt perfectly confident. All he had to do was wait.

* * *

The temperature had dropped quickly and the steel television tower glistened with a light coating of ice. Terry's woollen mitts stuck to the frosty bars; the tower crunched and cracked under his weight. But "practice makes perfect," his mom always said, and he landed safely on the ground.

The wind whipping at his face, Terry raced towards Bloor Street. He could hardly wait to tell Queenie the good news.

Darn, he thought, checking his pockets. He only had two-bits. That meant no treat to share with his friend. She would be disappointed, but the ice on the tower made him decide against going back.

Standing at the streetcar stop, his head tucked

into his collar and his hands deep in his pockets, he stamped around in circles trying to keep warm.

Suddenly the frozen air was splintered by the raucous clanging of fire-bells. Seconds later two fire trucks wheeled out of Station 14 and went squealing north on Ossington.

Terry took after them like a shot. From blocks away he could smell the acrid smoke and hear the fire's ominous roar. Pillars of flame were shooting into the sky like Roman candles, brilliant orange light bathed the heavens, and glowing embers flew through the air like a million sparklers on firecracker day.

Terry, hiding behind a clump of bushes, watched with burning admiration as two firefighters climbed to the top of the aerial ladder. Keeping their heads just below the billowing smoke, they trained a huge jet of water into a second storey window. When they finally came down from their dangerous perch their helmets and shoulders were shrouded in a thick layer of ice.

Fascinated as always by the fiery spectacle, Terry gradually moved out of his hiding place. All of a sudden a huge icy glove clamped down like a vice on his shoulder. He looked up and scarcely recognized the blackened face of Joe Hancock. In the bright firelight Terry could see that the edge of

Joe's ears were burned raw and his eyebrows and lashes were all singed off.

"What the hell are you doing here?" demanded Joe.

"Umm . . . my aunt sent me to the store and I got sidetracked," lied Terry.

Grabbing him roughly by the coat sleeve, Joe dragged him behind the bush. "You young fool!" he yelled above the tumult. "Lies won't help you now. Don't you realize what you're doing?"

"I'm watching the fire like all the other people here," Terry yelled back. "It's a free country, you know!" In spite of what Aunt Lottie said, he really liked the way that sounded.

Joe ignored it. "Well, all the other people here aren't suspected of arson. Now, this is your last chance. If I ever catch you within a mile of a fire again I'll turn you in myself . . . understand?" His grip tightened painfully on Terry's shoulder.

Wrenching himself free, Terry glared up at his one-time hero, the angry tears in his blazing eyes reflecting the fire. "It's you that doesn't understand, Joe. Haven't you heard the news? I've been exonerated." It was an exaggeration, he knew, but he didn't care. "If my dad was here I bet you wouldn't treat me like I was a criminal or something. My dad was as big as you . . . bigger! He could have beat you up with one hand tied behind his back!" he sobbed, dashing the hot tears from his eyes.

Scared that he'd gone too far, Terry turned and ran. Joe took after him, caught him by the collar, and spun him around.

For a split second they just stared at each other. Then Joe, his bloodshot eyes swimming too, grabbed his young friend and crushed him against his frozen coat. Terry heard the crack of leather and felt the stinging ice on his cheek.

Now the fireman held him out at arm's length. "I've got to get back there. My mates need me. But I want you to promise me something, Terry."

"Anything, Joe!"

"Then go home and wait for me. And promise me you won't run off again."

"I promise, Joe," cried Terry.

"All right. I'll see you soon, son. Real soon. You have my word on it." Then he plunged back into the inferno.

* * *

The next day the headlines in the Evening Telegram read: "Hero Firefighter Saves Girl." Terry read the story eagerly.

"A Toronto firefighter is a hero after last night's holocaust on Shaw Street. A small girl was trapped between collapsed floors of a residential building

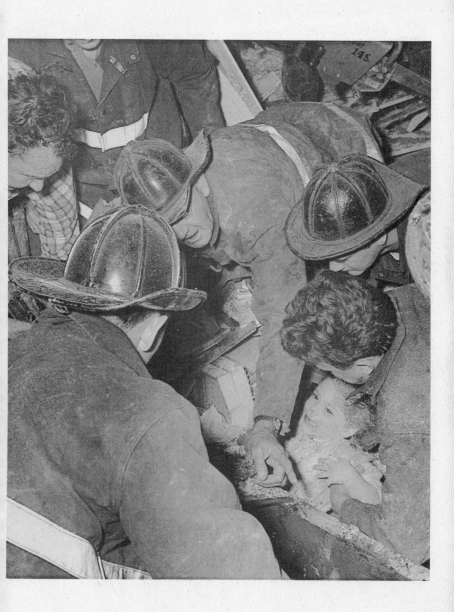

and Firefighter Joe Hancock risked his life to crawl through the smouldering wreckage and bring her out alive. Four-year-old Elisabeth Faber is recovering in the Hospital for Sick Children.

"Another fireman tragically lost his life in the blaze. Firefighter Bill Collins was blown off his extension ladder by an explosion. He was pronounced dead on arrival at Western Hospital."

Three days later the same newspaper carried the story of the funeral.

"Firefighter William Collins was laid to rest today with full Fire Department honours. The fire pumper which he had manned so often and so bravely was used as his caisson. Hundreds of his comrades from all over the province joined in the funeral procession which stretched for miles along Bloor Street.

"Thousands of mourners lined the sidewalks to pay their grateful respects and say a final farewell to a true Canadian hero."

Standing in the crowd at Ossington and Bloor, tears streaming down his face, stood Terry Dawson. As the caisson passed by, carrying the flag-draped coffin with the leather helmet riding proudly on top, Terry saluted. It was the only thing he could think of to do.

Chapter 18

Good as His Word

Two weeks passed and Terry had just about given up on Joe when the doorbell jangled so loudly it made everybody jump.

"Who in the world could that be?" Aunt Lottie complained irritably. She hated to be startled. Composing herself, she went to the door.

Terry slumped back down at the dining room table where he was working on a relief map of South America.

Cold air rushed in the moment the outside door was opened and Terry could hear the scraping of boots on the wire-mesh veranda mat.

"Is Terry home?" boomed a familiar voice.

Terry leapt up from the table, knocking the map askew in his hurry to get to the door.

"Hi, Joe!" he cried.

"Hi, there, Terry!"

Joe removed his hat and ran his fingers through his bushy brown hair. "Sorry I've taken so long to come by, but the department has been going crazy lately with chimney fires and coal-gas leaks and that big warehouse explosion down by the waterfront. Then just yesterday the water main on Dufferin broke and turned the street into an ice-rink."

As he spoke Aunt Betty came downstairs in her pink terry-cloth bathrobe, her fluffy fair hair done up in a forest of blue curlers. Upon recognizing their visitor she giggled self-consciously and tightened the strings of her bathrobe, giving the effect of an overstuffed pillow tied in the middle.

Aunt Lottie shot her a contemptuous glance which Aunt Betty simply ignored. She was doing that a lot lately, Terry had noticed.

Joe grinned at her in amusement, then turned to Aunt Lottie. "I hope I'm not disturbing you, ma'am. If it would be more convenient, I could come back tomorrow."

"You're not disturbing me in the least," sniffed Aunt Lottie as she did up the top button of her sensible black cardigan. "Some people are always dressed for company."

Embarrassed now, Aunt Betty excused herself

and scurried back upstairs as fast as her short legs would allow.

"Terence, take Mr. Hancock's coat," said Aunt Lottie.

Joe shrugged off his overcoat and pinched off his rubbers, each with the toe of the other foot. Terry hung the coat on the hall rack and they both followed Aunt Lottie into the living room.

Joe sat down on the velour chesterfield and made himself right at home. He placed a manila envelope on the occasional table. Terry sat down beside him.

"Well, son." Joe combed his moustache with his fingers.

Terry noticed that it had been trimmed neatly since the fire. "What have you been up to lately?"

"I'll show you." Beaming with pleasure at having his friend in the house, Terry ran and got his relief map from the dining room and spread it over the table, on top of the brown envelope.

Joe leaned forward and studied it intently. "It's terrific. You've done a fine job, Terry. Are you studying South America for geography class?"

Terry's face reddened as if he'd been found out. "Oh, no. Not particularly. I just like the terrain."

"School's going pretty well, then, is it?"

"Yeah. Not bad."

"Terence has been applying himself lately," put in Aunt Lottie unexpectedly. "It's bound to make a difference."

"Ah, but I always knew our boy was clever." Aunt Betty had returned, resplendent in a flowing pink muu muu. Her hair had been brushed into soft fair curls around her heart-shaped face, and she was wearing lipstick and rouge, too. She perched on the petit-point chair, the fullness of the gown puffed out around her like Aunt Lottie's doll-lamp. "My late brother, God rest his soul, was a chartered accountant, you know, a very clever man."

"Big fellow, too, I'm told." Joe grinned and Terry reddened some more.

"Yes, he was tall like his father and grandfather before him." Then, as an afterthought, she asked, "How tall are you, Mr. Hancock?"

"Oh, six foot one or two in my sock feet."

"Johnny, Terry's father, was six foot three," Aunt Betty prattled on. The firefighter's company seemed to bring out her natural vivacity. "We come from tall stock on the Dawson side. Charlotte takes after them. But I'm more like my dear little mother."

"I'm like my mother, too," said Terry proudly.

"You are indeed, dear." Aunt Betty leaned forward and smoothed the dark curls back from his forehead. "Your mother was lovely. My, how her brown eyes sparkled when she laughed." She sighed at the memory.

Not to be outdone, Aunt Lottie interjected, "Terence might favour his mother in looks, but he has his father's ways." Then she added in a more business-like tone, "May I ask the purpose of your visit, Mr. Hancock? Or is this just a social call?"

Joe smiled, showing white even teeth. "I guess you could say it's a little bit of both," he replied. "But, please, won't you call me Joe? I'm not used to this mister business."

"Oh, we will, we certainly will, won't we Charlotte?" chirped Aunt Betty. "And you must call me Elizabeth. No, not Elizabeth, that's much too formal. Call me Betty. Everyone says I look like a Betty . . . whatever that means."

"Betty it is then. A pretty name for a pretty lady."

Now it was Aunt Betty's turn to blush.

Charlotte Dawson cleared her throat impatiently. "For pity sakes, Elizabeth, let Mr. Hancock get to the point, if there is one."

But there was no stopping Aunt Betty now. "First we'll have tea. I made butter tarts this afternoon and they turned out delicious if I do say so myself. I hope you like butter tarts, Mr. . . . I mean, Joe."

"My favourite," Joe assured her, and Terry added, "Mine too!"

Aunt Lottie huffed again, then she picked up a *Woman's Day* magazine from the rack and began flipping the pages.

While Aunt Betty was bustling around in the kitchen, Joe and Terry studied the map of South America. Joe pointed to the city of Buenos Aires. "There's a place I'd like to see," he said.

"Me, too," agreed Terry.

At last Aunt Betty wheeled in the tea wagon and when everyone had been served, Aunt Lottie's patience finally gave out.

"Now," she set her teacup down with a sharp clink and stared straight at Joe, "I'd like to know what this is all about."

"Well . . . " Joe swallowed a bite of the gooey tart and washed it down with a gulp of tea. "I have a proposition to make, and I don't want your answer tonight. I want all three of you to sleep on it."

"What, Joe, what?" Terry felt a surge of excitement.

Joe wiped his mouth on the snowy napkin and set the cup on its matching saucer. Then he spoke directly to Terry. "Have you ever heard of an organization called Big Brothers?" he asked.

"No." Terry looked puzzled.

"I've heard of such an organization." Now Aunt Lottie began to show an interest, but Joe kept his eyes fixed on Terry.

"A Big Brother is a man who takes a special interest in a fatherless boy and helps him grow into manhood," he explained. "I've been a Big Brother to eight boys in the past twenty years, so you can see that I've had lots of practice."

Terry felt a stab of jealousy towards eight boys he'd never even heard of before.

"Mr. Hancock . . ." Aunt Lottie interrupted. Still miffed about being ignored, she waited until she had Joe's full attention before continuing, "What are you suggesting?"

Joe looked from her to Terry and their eyes locked. "That I become Terry's Big Brother, if he'll have me," he said.

Terry couldn't answer for the lump in his throat. He darted a pleading look at Aunt Lottie. He knew she would be the one to make the final decision.

"It sounds wonderful," chirped Aunt Betty in excitement, "and it's just what we need . . . a man around the house."

"Oh, for heaven's sake, Elizabeth, control yourself," snapped an embarrassed Aunt Lottie. Then she turned a solemn face towards Joe and Terry. If she says no, Terry thought, I'm leaving for South America tonight!

But Lottie didn't say no. "That's an interesting proposition, Mr. Hancock," she said cautiously. "But I'll need to know more about it."

"Of course. That's why I brought you this." Joe reached under the map for the manila envelope and handed it to Charlotte Dawson. "This is all the information you'll need right now. And, of course, I can produce the necessary references. Believe me, Miss Dawson, it's not easy to qualify to be a Big Brother."

Now he turned back to Terry, whose dark eyes were glowing. "The organization tries to match Big Brothers to Little Brothers according to their interests and personalities. I think you and I ought to make a good team, don't you, son?"

Again, because of the lump in his throat, Terry didn't trust himself to speak. He nodded his head vigorously and his smile stretched from ear to ear.

"Well!" Aunt Lottie stood up abruptly, signalling that the visit was over. "You'll certainly have your work cut out for you with Terence," she declared.

"That's what Big Brothers are for, ma'am," Joe answered evenly. Then he said goodnight and Terry walked with him to the door. "Thanks, Joe," he whispered. Joe just smiled.

Chapter 19

Brothers

The interviews with the Big Brothers went off without a hitch and in two short weeks, which seemed like forever to Terry, Joseph Matthew Hancock became official Big Brother to Terence Wendell Dawson.

That Saturday was Joe's day off, and he arrived bright and early at the house on Ossington. Terry was ready and waiting.

"What's the first thing you'd like to do?" Joe asked as Terry pulled on his rubber boots in the hall.

"I want to take you some place," Terry answered quietly.

"Some place?"

"Yep. It's a weird place. I hope you won't mind."

"You're the boss," Joe grinned and they went out the door together.

"Have fun, you two!" called Aunt Betty from the doorway.

They waved back at her as they walked to the street.

Joe's car, a new blue Ford Fairlane, was standing at the curb. They got in and Joe revved up the engine.

"Which way?" he queried.

"We've got to head west on Bloor Street," Terry said. Joe swung the car around in a U turn and made a left onto Bloor Street.

As they skidded along the streetcar tracks, Joe glanced over at his passenger. "How about filling me in on your family, Terry . . . your aunts and uncles and cousins."

Terry's dark eyes stared straight out the windshield. "I haven't got any uncles or cousins," he said dolefully. "My two aunts are the only relations I got."

Just then a streetcar clanged its warning bell, so Joe pulled off the tracks and came to a full stop behind the centre doors to let the passengers off safely.

"How about friends?" persisted Joe as he shifted into gear. "A good-looking guy like you must have a girlfriend."

Terry turned his head and looked out the side

window. "Nah. I'm kind of a loner. I used to be friends with a guy named Eric Thurston. But his mother killed that when I got in trouble. I don't care, though. I don't like him much, anyway."

"Tell me about your aunts," Joe persevered.

Terry began slowly. "My Aunt Lottie never wanted me. I thought it was because she hated me, but Aunt Betty says, no, it's because I remind her of my dad. My dad was the baby of their family and he was Aunt Lottie's favourite. But I don't see how I remind her of him because I look just like my mother. Here . . . I'll show you."

He reached inside his jacket and pulled a dog-eared snapshot out of his shirt pocket. It was a picture of a pretty woman, her head thrown back, laughing, the sun shining on a mass of curly dark hair.

He held it up, and Joe gave it a sidelong glance still keeping an eye on the road. "Yep. You're as alike as two peas in a pod. But maybe you take after your dad in other ways."

"That's what Aunt Betty says. She says that sometimes the expression on my face gives her a turn. Whatever that means."

Joe laughed, then became serious again. "You'll need to be patient with your Aunt Lottie, Terry. She'll come around in time. You'll see."

"Huh! She hasn't come around in a year and a half."

Joe's thick eyebrows drew together and his face went suddenly sad. "Some people mourn longer than others," he said.

Terry darted him a sharp glance and realized that Joe was thinking about his wife. Terry knew that she had died young, but he didn't know how. He quickly changed the subject. "Was your dad a fireman, too, Joe?"

"No, my dad was a steelworker, but my grandfather, Matthew Hancock, was a hero in the great Toronto fire of 1904. He was part of the fire brigade that stayed on duty for forty-eight hours and was credited with preventing the fire from spreading northward. They said the red glow in the sky could be seen as far north as Barrie. It was considered a miracle that nobody was killed."

"I bet he told you some great stories," Terry said enviously. "I wish I had a grandfather."

"One of these days I'll take you home with me and show you some of his mementos. Clippings from the paper and pictures of horse-drawn fire wagons. There's even a leather bucket he used in the bucket brigade."

"What was your most exciting fire, Joe?" Terry couldn't get enough of fire stories.

Joe stopped at a red light and put the clutch in neutral. He was silent until the light turned green, then he shifted into low and the car moved off.

"I don't know if exciting is the right word for it, Terry. Horrifying might be a better description."

"What?"

"It happened on September 17, 1949. Maybe it seems funny to remember so exactly, but it was one of those days that stays frozen in your mind as long as you live."

"What happened?" breathed Terry.

"That was the night the cruise ship Noronic burned at Pier 9 down on the waterfront." Joe's face grew tragic at the awful memory. "I'll never forget those charred bodies . . . 119 in all. And so many people scarred for life."

He passed a hand over his eyes as if to erase the gruesome picture. "I guess, in a strange way, you could call it exciting," he said with a shudder.

They both sat quietly for a while. Then Terry suddenly realized that they had reached the intersection of Bloor and Jane Streets and he craned his neck trying to catch a glimpse of Queenie's house. But it was too far away.

He hadn't seen Queenie for weeks now. Would she have forgotten him? He hadn't heard a word from her owners, so he guessed they had ignored his note. Or maybe it was still lying at the bottom of their mailbox.

"How much farther?" Joe inquired.

"A few miles," Terry answered.

They continued on without speaking until Terry said, "Turn left at the next corner."

His directions took them right through the stone gateway of Parklawn Cemetery.

Joe darted Terry a curious glance.

"Make a right here," Terry said.

Proceeding along a gravel road flanked on either side by row on row of marble gravestones, they saw two men digging a big oblong hole. Beside the hole the dirt was piled up like a giant ant-hill.

"Left!" Terry cried, then the next moment, "Stop!"

Joe braked and pulled off to the side of the road. The car leaned into the shallow ditch, and they got out.

Terry picked his way carefully between the monuments: stone angels, miniature churches, and crosses engraved with praying hands. Other markers lay flat on the ground like stepping stones.

Terry's rubber boots came to a standstill in front of a pink marble stone with a rounded top. Black scrolly letters were etched on the shiny surface. The graves it marked were covered with fresh, out-of-season flowers. With a pang Terry recognized Aunt Lottie's handiwork.

Joe took off his hat and held it over his heart. Terry did the same. "This here's my family," he whispered.

Joe read the inscription in a solemn voice: "In loving memory of John David Dawson, his wife, Carol Marie Wendell, and their young son, Albert John. May they rest in peace."

The man and the boy stood as still and silent as the grave itself.

Terry tried to picture them lying there. Where was Albert? Was the little white coffin on top of the mahogany one his mother was in, or his father's? Was he, Terry, standing at their head or their feet? Suddenly he wanted to know.

But his morbid imaginings were interrupted by the sudden, swift arrival of a fat spring robin. Landing on top of the headstone, he flicked his tail for balance, puffed out his orangey-red breast and began to chirrup with all his might.

"He's the first robin I've seen this year," Joe whispered.

"Me too!"

Terry forgot to whisper and scared the bird away. It flew to a nearby treetop and was joined almost instantly by a lighter coloured robin.

"That's probably the missus," Joe said, shading his eyes against the bright spring sun. "I'll bet they've got a nest somewhere and have started their family already."

Terry's gaze moved slowly from the birds above to the gravestone below. His eyes passed once more over the black letters, but the relentless singing of the robins drew his eyes to the blue sky again.

Suddenly he let out a snort of laughter. "You know what my mom did once?"

"No. What did she do?"

"She kidnapped a cat that was worrying a family of robins in our backyard. And she kept it in our cellar for about six days until all the baby birds were airborne. My dad called her a 'catnapper.' "

Joe laughed. "The cat must have gotten pretty hungry."

"Heck, no. She fed it. She even rigged up a litter box, and she let it sleep in the laundry basket."

"Lucky cat."

"The cat didn't think so. He was as mad as hops at Mom. Every time she went down the cellar he'd hiss at her and give her dirty looks. She always said if looks could kill she'd be dead . . . " He drew his breath in a gasp and stopped short. The smile dropped like a mask from his face.

Joe put his hat back on and rubbed his big hands

together. "It's getting cold out here. What say we find a restaurant and have a bite to eat?"

"Good idea." Terry turned quickly away from the grave and headed towards Joe's car. "I know where there's a swell fish-and-chip shop."

As they drove back along the gravel road they were met by a long black hearse moving at a snail's pace. A procession of cars, all with little black flags waving mournfully, followed in its wake. Joe pulled the Fairlane over to the shallow ditch and cut the engine respectfully.

The funeral cortege came to a halt by the muddy hole. The grave-diggers had retreated about fifty feet away. Leaning on their shovels, smoking cigarettes, they waited patiently to finish their job.

* * *

The aroma wafting out of the fish-and-chip shop door made Terry's mouth water. He realized as he walked in that it was the first time he had ever been in the place when he wasn't afraid of being caught.

He and Joe slid into a booth and took off their hats. Joe ran his fingers through his thatch of hair and Terry did the same. The fat woman in the greasy apron came over with her pencil and pad ready. She licked the pencil stub and gave Terry a friendly grin. "Hello, there, sonny," she said. "I see you brought your dad along this time."

Terry's heart skipped a beat and his breath caught in his throat.

Joe jumped into the breach. "Big Brother would be closer to the mark," he said. "What'll it be, Terry . . . french fries and double fish?"

"Swell," Terry agreed.

While they were waiting for their order, Terry decided to ask Joe something he had wondered about for a while.

"Have you got any kids, Joe?"

"No. That was one of the reasons I became a Big Brother. I like kids." Joe undid the top button of his shirt and loosened his necktie. Terry did the same. "I lived alone for two years after my wife died. Then, when my father passed away, I moved in with my mother. We help each other cope. It's hard when you lose your loved ones." He hadn't looked directly at Terry as he spoke, but now he glanced down and their eyes met. "How are you coping, son?" he said.

"I dunno." Terry felt tears washing under his eyelids so he quickly lowered them. "Sometimes I'm okay. But sometimes I wish I was dead too. Once I went out to the cemetery by myself on my bike and I laid down between the two graves to see if I'd fit. Then I shut my eyes and pretended I was with them. I stayed real still and held my breath for ages trying to feel dead. Then I ran out of breath and took a big loud snort of air and nearly scared the wits out of a lady walking by."

"That's one way of coping," Joe laughed.

Just then the piping hot food arrived and they both dove in with gusto.

Later, they went to the Lansdowne Theatre to see Bob Hope and Bing Crosby in a "Road" show. They rounded off the wonderful day by stopping at the White Corner restaurant for a hamburger and Coke. It was nine o'clock when they finally got back to the house on Ossington.

Aunt Betty met them at the door. "Come in, come in," she chirruped, sounding just like the robin. "You must be dying for a cup of tea."

Aunt Lottie, standing a few paces behind her sister, stretched out her arm and glanced at her gold wristwatch. "It's getting late," she said.

"Oh, fiddle!" cried Aunt Betty. "The night's young. Besides, it's Saturday. And I want to hear all about their day."

Joe's eyes twinkled as he laughed. Terry could tell he got a kick out of Aunt Betty. "Thanks just the same, Betty," he said. "But I'll have to take a raincheck this time. I go on duty at the firehall at midnight, so I'd better say goodnight now and head home to grab some shut-eye."

Then he looked over Aunt Betty's fluffy fair head

at her sister. "Goodnight to you, too, Lottie," he said. She smiled, a little stiffly, and nodded her head.

"See you, Terry!"

"See you, Joe! Thanks a lot!"

"Welcome!" Joe called back as he loped down the walk.

"Well, dear," Aunt Betty shut the door reluctantly. "Did you have a good time with your Big Brother?"

"Oh, we had a swell time, Aunt Betty." He hung up his jacket on the wall-rack. "First we went to the cemetery," his aunts exchanged a puzzled glance, "then we had fish and chips, then we went to the show. I'll bet Joe's the best Big Brother in the whole world."

He didn't tell them that after lunch he and Joe had driven up Jane Street, parked the car in front of Queenie's house, and walked together up the back lane. Behind the chain-link fence the yard looked vacant, and there was an emptiness about the place that made it seem deserted. Terry called and called Queenie's name, but she didn't answer.

That night, up in his attic room, Terry opened the top bureau drawer, slid his hand under the pile of clean shirts and brought out the picture of his family. He switched on the green bottle lamp on the night table and laid the picture under it.

Terry gazed for a long time at each beloved face. With his index finger he traced the outline of their well-remembered features. Then, because he was alone, and no one would ever know, he kissed them through the glass.

Chapter 20

Re-united

One warm spring day in May Aunt Lottie appeared unexpectedly at lunchtime, much to Aunt Betty's annoyance. That meant she wouldn't be able to watch her favourite soap-box story, "Search for Tomorrow." Her sister disapproved of wasting the picture tube on "trash."

Aunt Lottie had brought the morning mail in with her and began sifting through it as she ate her finnan-haddie. She put her fork down and held one letter up to the window, squinting her eyes in an effort to see through the envelope.

"What have you got there, Charlotte?" asked Aunt Betty.

Terry paid no attention and continued to eat ravenously. The mail never had anything to do with him, anyway. But this day he was in for a surprise.

"It's a letter for Terence," Aunt Lottie said with a puzzled frown. "It's postmarked Vancouver."

"Vancouver?" Terry dropped his fork with a clatter, grabbed the envelope, and slit it open with his table knife. He unfolded a single sheet of notepaper and began to read. As he read the black hairs on the back of his neck curled up and his brown eyes grew as big as agates.

"Holy cow!" he cried.

"I beg your pardon?" snapped Aunt Lottie.

"What is it, Terry? What's happened?" begged Aunt Betty.

In answer he handed her the letter. But before she had a chance to read one word, Aunt Lottie snatched it out of her hand.

She scanned the page so slowly that Aunt Betty became fidgety and began tearing a piece of bread apart. Finally Aunt Lottie condescended to read the letter out loud, beginning with the address in the top right-hand corner.

44 Park St., Apt. 703,
Vancouver, B.C.,
May 9, 1956
Dear Terry Dawson,

You will no doubt be surprised to receive this letter, so let me introduce myself. I am the owner of the German shepherd dog

*known as "Queenie" whom you seem well
acquainted with . . .*

Aunt Lottie darted Terry a quizzical look over
her glasses.

>*. . . I still have the note you left in my
mailbox in Toronto. You will notice by the
above address that my wife and I have relo-
cated. This is why I am writing to you.*

>*Dogs are not allowed in our apartment
building and we see no possibility of getting
a house in the near future. In the meantime
Queenie is being boarded at the Canine Kennels on Roncesvalles Avenue in Toronto. She
has been there over a month and the kennel
owner, Mr. K. Arliss, informs me that she is
very lonely, cries continuously, and is not
eating well.*

>*Do you still want her, as your note indi-
cates? If so, and you can give her a good
home, then the enclosed letter to Mr. Arliss,
along with a cheque for her keep, will release
her into your custody.*

>*Please advise me quickly by return mail.
If we can't find a home for Queenie soon it
may be necessary to have her put down.*

>>*Yours truly,*
>>*William A. Hanks, Esq.*

Aunt Lottie rattled the paper under Terry's nose. "Explain!" she demanded.

"Well . . . " He lowered his eyes and kept them glued to his plate. "She's just a dog I used to talk to on my way home from school." He had the fingers of both hands crossed underneath the table. If only Aunt Lottie wouldn't ask him any more questions.

Before she had a chance, Aunt Betty broke in and saved the day. "Do you remember Sheppie, Charlotte?" She asked in a tremulous voice.

Terry glanced up curiously just in time to see a fleeting expression of sadness pass over Aunt Lottie's face.

"Yes, I remember Sheppie," she answered very quietly.

"Who was Sheppie?" Terry whispered to Aunt Betty.

This time Aunt Lottie interrupted.

"His name was Shepherd, since he was a German shepherd," she glanced at the letter in her hand, "like Mr. Hanks' dog, Queenie." She paused just long enough for Aunt Betty to jump in again.

"Sheppie belonged to your father when he was a little boy, Terry. Oh, how Johnny loved that dog. We all did, didn't we, Charlotte?"

Aunt Lottie nodded her head slowly. "I'll never

forget the day he got killed by the milkman's wagon," she murmured.

"Sheppie got killed!" cried Terry.

"I just said so, didn't I?" Aunt Lottie scowled at her nephew. "I wouldn't be likely to make up such a story." Arranging her knife and fork in a cross on her plate she continued, "John mourned that dog so deeply that father went to the pound and got him another one. A part shepherd, she was. But John didn't take to her."

"Her name was Polly," Aunt Betty reminisced, her blue eyes damp, "and she was lovely. Since Johnny didn't take to her she became my pet."

"Are there any pictures of Sheppie?" asked Terry.

"I believe so." Aunt Betty got right up and hurried to the sideboard in the dining room where the brown leather album was kept.

Aunt Lottie cleared a place on the kitchen table and Aunt Betty opened it in front of her. Aunt Lottie wet her thumb and turned a few pages. Then she stopped suddenly, her finger resting at the edge of a yellowed snapshot, held in place with little black cardboard triangles at each corner. It showed a small boy kneeling beside a big German shepherd, his face buried in the thick ruff of her neck.

The dog looked so much like Queenie that it

brought a rush of hope to Terry's heart.

"You'd like Queenie, Aunt Lottie," he began breathlessly. "She's real friendly, but she's a good watchdog, too."

At this, his aunt shut the album abruptly and shoved it aside. "Dogs are messy creatures to have around the house," she said.

"Not Queenie!" declared Terry. "She's an outdoor dog. She's always lived outdoors in the back shed in Mr. Hanks' yard. I bet I could make a swell home for her in our back shed. And I'll bet Joe would help me, too."

"Oh, what do you say, Charlotte?" Aunt Betty was beside herself with excitement. "It would be a treat to have a dog in the family again."

They both held their breath while Aunt Lottie frowned and thought. Finally she spoke. "Perhaps we could ask Mr. Hancock if he would fetch the dog in his car. After all, we can't sit by and let it be destroyed. But I will only agree to it if the creature remains outside at all times."

Terry let out a whoop of joy and raced up to the firehall.

* * *

The next Saturday Joe and Terry went to the Canine Kennels on Roncesvalles. Joe handed Mr. Hanks' letter to the receptionist at the desk.

She read it through. "Are you Terry Dawson?" she asked Joe.

"No, the lad here is Terry Dawson. I'm Joe Hancock, Terry's Big Brother."

She twirled in her swivel chair and got up. "I'll take this letter to Mr. Arliss," she said, and disappeared down a long corridor towards the rear of the building.

An elderly man in a wrinkled smock returned with her, reading the letter. With his fingers he combed thin strands of grey hair across his shiny pink head. His half spectacles slid down and stopped short at the bulb on the end of his nose.

Tapping the letter with a stubby finger, he said, "This is the German shepherd that's been pining away for weeks now. I was just about to get in touch with the owner to suggest that it might be kinder to put her to sleep."

Terry's stomach knotted and his heart banged in his chest. "Where is she?" he asked anxiously.

"I'll get her. Be back in a jiffy."

The old man ambled down the hall again. A moment later he returned, tugging a whimpering dog at the end of a leash. Her long pointed ears lay flat against her head and her straggly tail curled dejectedly between her hind legs.

"Queenie!" Terry cried.

The dog stopped dead. At first she seemed not to believe her eyes.

"It's me, Queenie, Terry. I've come to take you home."

Suddenly her ears sprang up and she howled like a wolf. With a mighty bound she broke free of the leash. Leaping on Terry, she knocked him down and they rolled on the floor in a joyous reunion.

The kennel owner raised his voice to make himself heard over the ruckus. "Not so fast there, young man. I'll need proof of your identity, and your parents' consent. I can't just release a dog to any Tom, Dick or Harry who walks in off the street with a letter in his hand."

Now Terry and Queenie stood close together. Sensing something wrong, Queenie pressed her thin body against Terry. He could feel her ribcage right through his pant leg.

"I don't have any parents," Terry said. "I live with my aunts. But they said I could have her. You can phone them."

"Hold on a minute." Joe put his hand on Terry's shoulder. "Let me handle this." He fished his wallet from his back pocket, took out his Fire Department identification card and handed it to Mr. Arliss.

"The boy has no identification with him," Joe explained, "But I can vouch for the fact that his aunts have given him their permission to bring the dog home."

Mr. Arliss looked at Joe's card, peering at his photograph in the Fire Department's navy-blue dress uniform. Then he looked up. "This is good enough for me."

Handing the card back to Joe, he put the leash in Terry's hand.

"You're a lucky lady," he told Queenie, giving her head a pat.

"Heck no, I'm the lucky one," Terry said as he fastened the leash to Queenie's collar. "I've got me the best dog in the universe."

Joe's moustache stretched from ear to ear as he shook hands with Mr. Arliss. Then he opened the door and led the way back to his car.

* * *

Terry and Joe made Queenie a clean, comfortable home in the back shed and she had the run of the yard. In no time at all she was healthy again, and she acted as if she'd lived there all her life.

Chapter 21

Red-handed

On warm summer nights, Terry left his dormer window wide open for fresh air. He drifted in a contented sleep.

Suddenly he woke with a start. He sat bolt upright in bed, his eyes staring into the darkness, his heart going like a trip-hammer.

Automatically he reached for the lamp switch. Then his hand stopped in mid-air. Instead, he got up in the dark and crept across the floor to the open window.

The leaves rustling on the oak tree were not thick enough yet to block his view, and the empty house across the road was plainly visible by the street lamp.

It was the old Thatcher place and, as Aunt Lottie constantly complained, it was an eyesore. No wonder, she said, that the Thatchers could neither rent nor sell it. The only sign that anyone had ever lived there was a bedraggled curtain still drooping inside the bay window.

Suddenly a small, bright light flared in the window, flickered like a match, then went out. Instantly it re-appeared and began wavering, ghost-like, back and forth.

Cold shivers traced Terry's spine. "Geez, maybe it's him!" he whispered to himself, rushing out of his room. In his hurry he tripped over the shoes he'd kicked off carelessly and almost took a header down the attic stairs.

First he tapped on Aunt Lottie's closed door. "Wake up, Aunt Lottie," he called in a hoarse whisper. Then he ran down the hall to Aunt Betty's room. "Come quick, Aunt Betty."

Aunt Lottie's door flew open and she emerged in the semi-darkness, hastily tying her housecoat around her lanky body. Aunt Betty came scurrying in her filmy nightdress, a toilet-paper turban floating out behind her.

"For mercy sakes, Terence, what's gotten into you?" snapped Aunt Lottie irritably. "It must be the middle of the night."

Terry ran past her into the forbidden room and flung up the blind so hard it fluttered wildly at the top. Aunt Lottie's room overlooked the street, so she had a perfect view of the Thatcher place.

"Turn the lights on, Elizabeth," commanded Aunt Lottie.

"No!" protested Terry. "Come and look out first. I want you to see something."

The two women crept up behind him and peered over his shoulders.

"What is it, Terry? What are we looking for?" whispered Aunt Betty.

"I saw lights over there. Like somebody was striking matches."

"Well, I don't see a thing," said Aunt Lottie.

"Neither do I," Aunt Betty had to agree.

"You will. He'll light another one any second."

"Who in the world are you talking about?" snapped Aunt Lottie.

"The firebug. I'm sure it's the firebug." Terry's voice was trembling with excitement.

They held their breaths and waited, but the empty house across the street just stood there looking like a big black box.

"This is ridiculous." Aunt Lottie reached up with a long arm and pulled the blind back down to the sill. "It's all in your imagination."

"No! There's a guy over there striking matches!"

"Stop your nonsense and get up those stairs to

bed," ordered Aunt Lottie as she shoved Terry and her sister back into the hall and slammed the door.

"Away you go, Terry," yawned Aunt Betty as she rewound her turban and fastened it with a bobby pin. "You're just overwrought, thinking about that firebug all the time. You let the Fire Department worry about him. Goodnight, dear." She kissed him lightly on the forehead. "Sleep tight."

Terry realized it was useless to argue, so he stomped back up the stairs and went straight to the dormer window. One glance told him he was right. There it was again, a trembling but unmistakable match light.

Dressing in a flash, he went out the back window. He rushed down the tower, heedless of the grating noise it always made, and headed for the back shed.

"Shhh, Queenie," he said in a warning whisper. "Be quiet, it's just me . . . Terry."

He lifted the latch. Queenie didn't make a sound, but her hair was standing on end like porcupine quills and her whole body quivered with excitement.

Taking a firm grip on her collar, he led her through the alleyway to the street. Terry looked up at the window again and saw a shadow moving in the flickering light.

Together they raced like the wind to the fire-hall.

"Help, somebody, help!" cried Terry, pounding on the firehouse door.

Luck was with him. Joe Hancock rolled up the wide red door.

"What the . . . !" exclaimed Joe, his big frame silhouetted in the doorway. "Terry! What are you doing here? It's two o'clock in the morning."

"I think I've found him, Joe. The firebug! He's torching the old Thatcher house right this minute. If we hurry we can catch him in the act."

"Why didn't you sound the alarm?"

"I didn't want to warn him, Joe. I want to catch him."

Without further explanation, Joe alerted the other firemen and called the police. "No lights, no sirens," he directed. "We've got a chance to nab this guy red-handed."

Jumping into the cab of the waiting fire truck, he signalled Terry and Queenie to jump in beside him. Two firefighters slid down the pole, grabbed their coats and helmets from the wall, and hopped onto the back of the moving truck.

They proceeded quietly down Ossington Avenue. When they stopped in front of the Thatcher house it was in total darkness.

"Oh, no!" Terry thought in dismay. "Now Joe won't believe me either!"

But suddenly the curtains went up in a wave of flames and the bay window became a blazing fireplace. The firemen sprang into action.

With the dog's collar in a firm grip, Terry slipped down the alleyway between the two houses. Behind him he heard the shattering of glass, the rush of water, and the pungent smell of smoke.

But all he could think about was the firebug. Terry was sure the man would try to make his escape out the back way. And he was right. With a bang the back door of the house flew open and a shadowy figure ran thudding down the yard to launch himself at the high board fence.

"Go get him, Queenie!" Terry yelled as he let go of her collar. Like a bolt of lightning she streaked down the yard. In one mighty bound she grabbed the fugitive by the pant leg and brought him crashing to the ground. Straddling his quivering body with all four paws, she growled, revealing her drooling white fangs and snarling at every move he made.

Within moments the police arrived. One officer shone his flashlight into the man's horrified face. "You can call your dog off now, son. We'll take over from here," he said.

"Not until this guy confesses," Terry replied stubbornly. And Queenie continued to snap her teeth just inches from the terrified man's nose.

"I give up!" blubbered the man like a baby. "I set it! I'm the guy you've been looking for! Oh, please, call off the wolf and take me to jail!"

He sounded so pitiful Terry almost felt sorry for him. "Here, Queenie," he called, and she came to him obediently.

Then the police took over. Handcuffing the hapless arsonist, they dragged him to his feet and shoved him ahead of them through the alleyway. Terry and Queenie followed at their heels.

With hanging head and hands shackled behind his back, the arsonist scrambled into the safety of the police car.

As the cruiser pulled away, the district fire chief emerged from the smoky house and declared the emergency over. The firefighters boarded up the window and locked the doors, and the hose was quickly reeled back onto the truck as the chief drove off.

Captain Forrest came over to Terry. "Well, son," he said in a hearty voice. "That fellow's confession sure lets you off the hook. And that's a mighty fine dog you've got there. He leaned down and gave Queenie a pat on the head and she wagged her tail profusely. Terry just about burst with pride.

By now the street was full of curious onlookers. In spite of the fact there had been no sirens, the general commotion had awakened most of the neighbourhood. Suddenly Terry had a funny feeling that he was being watched. He glanced over his shoulder and, sure enough, there stood his aunts on the lighted veranda.

"Uh, oh. I think I'm in trouble," he said to Joe.

Joe followed his gaze and laughed. "You tell them that your Big Brother says you and your dog are heroes. And you'd better get a hero's welcome or I'll know the reason why."

Terry waited until the fire truck had left and the crowd dispersed before reluctantly crossing the street.

Before his aunts could say a word, he bounded up the steps and burst out, "The guy confessed! When Queenie had him down he admitted to starting all the fires in the neighbourhood. And Captain Forrest says that proves I'm not the firebug. And Joe says Queenie and me are heroes!"

Then he turned to his Aunt Betty. "A hero shouldn't have to live outside in an old shed," he said. "Couldn't Queenie be a house dog now and sleep on the mat in my room?"

Aunt Betty hesitated, darting a questioning

glance at her sister. Terry and Queenie looked anxiously from one to the other.

Aunt Lottie frowned and stared at the two heroes. There was a long pause. At last she spoke. "Well . . . if you can promise me that there'll be no muddy paw-prints all over my house . . . and that you'll take full responsibility for her care . . . and . . ."

Terry broke in with an unbelieving gasp, "Do you mean it, Aunt Lottie? Really?"

His Aunt Lottie's frown slowly gave way to a smile. "Terence," she said, "When did you ever hear me say something I didn't mean?"

With a jubilant cry Terry dropped to his knees and buried his face in the thick ruff of Queenie's neck.

And from that moment on, the house on Ossington was home.

Epilogue

The Firefighters at Station 14 honoured Terry with a framed poem for his part in the capture of the firebug.

> *FIREMEN*
> *Here's to fire fighters all!*
> *Always at your beck and call!*
> *Vigilant and unafraid . . .*
> *Volunteer or city paid!*
> *Scientific men are these,*
> *Fighting fire . . . a dread disease . . .*
> *Challenging a flaming hell*
> *At the ringing of a bell!*
> *Unknown heroes clad in blue*
> *They give up their lives for you!*
> *Pray for them as they go past*
> *Every ride may be their last.*
> *— Author Unknown*

Bernice Thurman Hunter is one of Canada's most popular children's writers. She is best known for her Booky trilogy — stories about growing up during the Great Depression. The first in the series, *That Scatterbrain Booky,* won the 1981 IODE Award and has been made into an award-winning musical.

Bernice's other books include the Margaret series, about a girl and her beloved horse, and *Lamplighter,* which paints an authentic picture of life in Northern Ontario during the 1880s. Her most recent best-seller is *The Railroader,* the exciting adventures of a boy in the late 1940s who dreams of becoming a railroad engineer.

In 1990, Bernice Thurman Hunter won the Vicky Metcalf Award for her contribution to Canadian children's literature. She continues to write stories about days gone by, and enjoys visiting schools and libraries to meet her readers.